MY BEAUTIFUL NEIGHBOR

PIPER RAYNE

Cover Photo: Wander Aguiar Photography

Cover Design: By Hang Le

1st Line Editor: Joy Editing

2nd Line Editor: My Brother's Editor

Proofreader: My Brother's Editor

My Beautiful Neighbor

Who's the mystery woman who just walked into my brewery?

I'm not the only one from my Alaskan small town asking themselves that question. But I'm positive, I'm the only one in Sunrise Bay undressing the pretty blonde in my head. Everything about her, from her make-up to her high heels says she's a fish out of water.

Whispers and speculations run rampant until the secret of who she is gets uncovered. Then the rumor mill goes into overdrive when she announces she's staying to open a book-store in the building next to mine—throwing a big wrench into my plans to buy that empty building.

I quickly find myself in a tug-of-war since my business partner/brother is upset she's ruined the opportunity to expand our business. I try to keep my distance, but I've got one sister with a gossip column on the local radio station and two meddling grandmas setting me up as a tour director.

And now I kind of like the idea of our new neighbor staying. But small-town life isn't for the weak—time will tell if she has what it takes to be one of us.

My Beautiful
NEIGHBOR

The Greenes

Hank's Kids
Cade Greene (30)
Co-owner Truth or Dare Brewery
Fisher Greene (28)
Sheriff
Xavier Greene (26)
Pro Football Player
Adam Greene (24)
Forest Ranger
Chevelle Greene (23)
Water Boat Tourist

Marla's Kids
Jed Greene (30)
Co-owner of Truth or Dare Brewery
Nikki Greene (27)
Radio Host
Mandi Greene (25)
Owner of SunBay Inn
Posey Greene (21)
Owner of Fringe

Hank and Marla's Kid
Rylan Greene (10)

Chapter One

"And the plot thickens."
- Nikki Greene

Cade

"Sure, I'll just jump over the casket, interrupting the entire service, and say, 'Hey, sorry about your mom, but her store? How much do you want for it?'" I whisper to my step-brother, Jed.

"I meant after the service is done. I'm not a complete asshole."

I cock my eyebrow, and he snickers. My dad turns around and gives us his classic glare. The one that says, "shut the hell up." We both shove our hands in the pockets of our slacks and bow our heads.

Once the prayer is over, the preacher says, "Amen."

Everyone stands straighter, and low whispers from the population of Sunrise Bay sound on the light breeze, all directed to Clara Harrison over the loss of her mother.

Jed and I walk down the hill from the cemetery together because Clara decided to hold her mother's wake at our brewery for some reason, which means we have to get over there to open it and make sure everything is ready to go.

"I'm simply suggesting you ask a question," he says, climbing into his truck.

"Then you do it," I say.

"Why would I ask when she's *your* brother's best friend?"

"Don't forget, she's *your* stepbrother's best friend."

Jed always uses the whole "your brother" or "your sister" thing when he doesn't want to do something. I don't see him saying he's not his brother when he uses the fact that Xavier is a pro football player to try to pick up women. And I didn't see him decline the tickets to watch a game from a box suite when Xavier offered them.

"You've known her your entire life," he argues, then pulls away from the curb.

"Which makes it all that much more insensitive." He is not going to win this argument.

We wave to the rest of our family coming down the hill to reach their vehicles. Xavier's arm is wound tightly around Clara's shoulders. I feel her pain. Hell, my gaze lingers as we pass my mother's burial plot, and I get that stabbing sensation in my heart like I do every time I see it—even if it has been eighteen years. The healing process can be long and difficult, but she'll get through it like I did at the age of twelve.

"You realize that Chuck on the other side wants to expand as well. We have to use any advantage we have."

Jed's not wrong. It's one of the reasons why our partnership in Truth or Dare Brewery has worked. In business, Jed thinks long-term while I think short term. I plan fun trivia nights and I'm concerned about the customers we have now enjoying themselves, while his goal is for our beer to be in every grocery store and bar in the nation. It works for us.

I know he's right, that I need to get to Clara first. I don't think she'll want to do anything with her mom's old sewing store next door to our brewery, but who can say for sure? I have to persuade her to sell us the space so we can knock down the wall and expand the brewery. And I will talk to her—just not on Jed's timeline.

But Jed also isn't a Sunrise Bay lifer, so maybe that's why we see things differently. Sure, he's been here since he was seventeen when his mom fell in love with my dad, blending our two families together, but then we went off to college. Jed forgets that Sunrise Bay is a small Alaskan town that takes care of their own. If I approach Clara today, gossip will spread that I'm an insensitive asshole. And it'd be right.

"I know. Don't worry, I'll talk to her, but not today," I say.

"I don't see the problem with a question like 'are you into sewing?' I mean, what do we know about Clara, other than she wants to nail Xavier?"

I scrunch my eyebrows. "They're best friends. *Platonic* best friends."

He laughs. "You're insane if you really think that. She knows his stats better than he does. She makes you organize those nights at the brewery for him every time he plays. She paints his number on both of her cheeks. She wants him."

"I don't know. I never got that impression that she liked him in that way."

Jed shakes his head, pulling into the back lot of the brewery. "This is why you need to get out there."

I climb out of his truck, shedding my suit jacket immediately. It's early spring, so it's still a bit chilly, but I'd rather deal with the cold than the confines of wearing a suit. "Out where?"

"Out in the dating world."

Unlike Jed, I rarely go outside of Sunrise Bay. When we graduated from college and got the loan to start the brewery, I put everything I had into it, wanting it to be a success. I had girlfriends in college, but I always knew I was coming back here to my hometown of Sunrise Bay, Alaska. I didn't want to live anywhere else, and not every woman wants to live in a small town this far north. That's not to say I'm celibate either, but my family doesn't need to know all my business, even though they think they do.

We walk into the brewery, flipping on the lights. I head to the front door, unlock it, and put out the chalkboard sign that states we're closed for a private party. Mrs. Harrison's sewing store is next door, dark and abandoned. I'm not sure the last time it was open. When Mrs. Harrison was first diagnosed, Clara tried to keep up the store in the hopes that her mom would beat the disease and could come back to it. But unfortunately, she didn't so now it sits in the middle of our main square, looking like it went out of business.

I walk over and fix the awning that flipped up from the wind last night, but there's no hiding the fading and ripped navy material. Our wonderful mayor, Sam Klein, put in a mandate for all the businesses in the square to have matching awnings to make us look uniform. One of his many annoying mandates.

Our square portion of downtown is pedestrian-friendly. It's literally a square with all the parking at the backs of the buildings. Cobblestone streets separate the shops from one side to the other, and during tourist season, white string lights are hung from one side of the road to the other. During the holiday season, it's colored lights paired with long strips of garland. Sunrise Bay is as charming as any town I've ever seen, and I'm lucky to call it home.

On my way back into the brewery, my eyes catch sight

of a blonde sitting on the park bench in the open area next to The Grind. She's dressed in funeral attire—black pants and black heels. I can't see her shirt since her black coat is covering it. She must be a guest, maybe waiting for others to arrive. There's something familiar about her, though I can't place her. Maybe if she'd look up from her phone, I'd stand a better chance.

"That's her," Nikki says, and I glance over my shoulder to see my stepsisters Nikki and Mandi stopped right outside of the brewery. "Who is she?"

Mandi shrugs. "She was at the funeral."

I walk over to them. "Is that why she looks familiar? Is she from around here?"

Because Sunrise Bay is small, if you don't know the person, you at least recognize them. Since we're not in the middle of tourist season, seeing outsiders is unusual—unless they're from a neighboring town like Lake Starlight. But if she was at the funeral, that would mean she knows the Harrisons.

"Maybe she was a customer," I offer.

Nikki scoffs, but that's Nikki. She's always looking for a more clandestine angle. "No way. You're telling me that girl sews?"

"What?" I ask. I mean, my little sister, Chevelle, went through that phase when she tried to make her own clothes after she heard how manufactured fabric could be toxic. "Why not?"

"Look at her clothes. Her nails? Her hair? It's all done to perfection. I'd bet money she's not a customer, which means it's something else..." Nikki taps her lips with her own perfectly manicured nails. Takes one to know one, I suppose.

"Try not to make your story too far from the truth," I say, walking into the brewery.

"Hey," she says, following me, "I always tell the truth in my segments."

"Sure you do." I grab a tray of wings from one of our servers to arrange it on the tables we pushed together along the back wall for a buffet-style pick-and-go.

"I take that as an insult," she says as she walks away.

As if small town gossip isn't enough, my stepsister has decided to fill everyone in on the buzz during her morning radio show. You know, just in case someone happened to miss it.

A few more people are in here now, all shedding their coats as they find a table. We've set our two most popular beers in the middle of each with glasses to share.

Xavier walks Clara in. She's holding up surprisingly well. Coming from such a big family, I can't imagine being the last family member alive. Her dad died in a fishing accident that killed five men six years ago, her grandma died thirteen years ago, and now her mom. Since she's an only child, she doesn't have anyone else.

But I'm not too worried about her. As Xavier goes to fix her a plate, my stepmom, Marla, grabs Clara's hands and squeezes, leading her to a table. The Greenes will pick her up as one of our own.

For some reason, my gaze is pulled back to the park bench. The woman isn't there anymore. Turning toward the room, I scour the guests, recognizing pretty much everyone. No sign of her.

"It might be good news for Clara. Maybe it's an aunt or something. Some long-lost relative," I overhear Nikki talking to her best friend, Molly.

"Molly should be working," I say. "Not listening to your absurd theories about some woman minding her own business on a park bench."

Molly fills a pitcher and hands it over to another server to deliver.

Nikki puts up her hand as if we're thirteen. "I can talk to my best friend. Stay out of it."

"Yeah, A and B conversation," Molly jokes. "C your way out of it."

"Funny. I'm paying your best friend, so for the next two hours, she's not your accomplice in churning gossip."

I'm not sure why I have such a dislike for the gossip of a small town. I mean, I chose to come back here after college knowing the score—there's no privacy. But finding out that my dad was sleeping with his cousin's ex-wife from someone other than him back when I was seventeen left a mark. Even if it all worked out and he's now married to her and I gained four stepsiblings and one half-sibling. Talk about having our lives spotlighted in this town. With spotlights come expectations.

"There's my grandson." Grandma Ethel hugs me, barely meeting me chest level. "I was just telling Dori that I hope to be dancing at your wedding soon."

I roll my eyes inwardly because if I did it outright, Grandma Ethel would pinch me like she used to when I was little. It doesn't matter that I'm thirty now. But these are the kinds of expectations I was talking about.

"Doubtful," I say. I'm not going to sugarcoat the fact that they might never get their way. I'm not playing into their expectations.

Being the eldest Greene means everyone wants to know when I'm going to settle down. Jed is the same age as I am, but everyone knows Jed is at least five years from being ready to settle down, so I'm somehow being pushed into dating so I can procreate. "Carry on the name," George from Handyman Haven told me last week. "You don't want to die alone," someone else said. And the best one yet, "Your mom would want to see you settled with a family." That one came from Zoe at The Grind. The kicker is that she was my mom's business partner, so maybe she actually knows what my mom would've wanted for all of us.

"Oh, Ethel, let him be. When he finds the right one, he'll know. From my experience, it happens when you least expect it. You never know who your forever is until you do," Dori Bailey says.

I rock back on my heels and nod. Usually she and my grandma are thick as thieves, so I'm surprised she's telling my grandma to lay off. I've heard the rumors about Dori and the way she manipulated all her grandchildren. Not happening on my watch.

"All he needs is to get laid!" Jed claps me on the shoulder.

"Jed Greene!" Grandma Ethel scolds, but he laughs and kisses her cheek.

"Looking good, Bibi."

Grandma Ethel's eyes flash with adoration. Since Jed already has two grandmas, he calls Grandma Ethel, Bibi, which is Swahili. Only Jed could get away with something like that. Him and his charismatic personality win over everyone.

He looks at me. "Did you ask Clara yet?"

I open my mouth to answer, but a silence falls over the room.

"And the plot thickens," Nikki whispers from my other side.

I turn toward the door as the blonde from the park bench steps into the brewery. I swear a stiff breeze follows her, alerting all of us that something big is about to happen.

Chapter Two

"Did you know Mrs. Harrison?"
– Cade Greene

Presley

I step into the brewery where the wake is being hosted and silence descends as if I'm the wicked witch of the east.

Mom warned me this would happen. She was desperate to come with me to Sunrise Bay, but I told her I could handle this myself. "You don't understand small towns. You're not going to be welcomed with open arms," she said.

In some ways, I'm grateful to have an overprotective mother. In other ways, I think it took my dad strapping Mom to a chair for her not to be behind me right now, saying I told you so.

I offer a small smile and my eyes fall to the daughter, Clara. She's been huddled with people the entire service and continues to be now. I figured maybe people would drink, eat, and retell happy stories about her mother, staying distracted enough that I could seek out Clara and talk to her.

Instead of doing what I intended before all attention was on me, I beeline it over to the refreshments with the hopes they'll forget I'm here. I grab a small plate. I'm not really hungry, but I can't very well stand here and not drink or eat, expecting people not to notice.

After I find a spot in the corner, blocked by a group of four having a conversation about some town competition that doesn't pertain to me, I sit quietly and wait for my opportunity.

A guy comes by, already filling my cup. "Want a drink?"

He's cute. Short dark hair and a little bit of scruff, but still clean-cut. Arms inked with tattoos, and he flashes me the smile that's probably gotten him in a lot of women's panties.

"Oh, no." I hold up my hand, but he pushes the filled cup my way regardless.

"It's my specialty, so I'd be offended if you didn't try it." He uses his toe to pull out a stool before having a seat.

I look over his shoulder to see half the people in the brewery staring at us.

"Ignore them. Nosy small-town people with nothing better to do." He waves off the people, but that doesn't stop them from staring.

This guy screams attention, and I want anything but that right now.

"I'm Jed. Jed Greene." He puts out his hand.

I shake it and his gaze falls down my body as though it should ignite me into flames. Either my libido crashed when I landed in this small town, or this guy isn't that hot. I think it might be the former because on a regular day, I'd definitely find him attractive. But not on a day when I have to do what I'm here to do.

"Hi, Jed Greene." I shake his hand. He waits for me to offer my name, but I take a sip of the beer to dodge the question. I raise the glass. "This is good."

He winks as though he already knew that. Cocky usually does it for me, but still nothing. Then the room grows louder, and I glance over his shoulder again, finding no one staring at us, except for one guy. The guy from outside who was talking to the two girls earlier. He's speaking with someone, but his gaze flickers over to Jed and me a few times.

"So, mystery girl. Just so you know, there are a lot of theories being thrown around."

"About?"

He chuckles so loudly, the person behind us looks over. "About who you are. I'm the unofficial town representative."

I tilt my head. "To find out who I am?"

He looks around. "Yeah. I can be the welcome man too, if you like."

"Welcome man?" I question.

This guy is definitely used to getting any woman on her back with minimal effort, and he clearly thinks he's going to accomplish that with me. As much as sex with a stranger sounds amazing right now—because it would clear my mind —I have no interest.

"You know how there's the welcome wagon..."

I scrunch my eyebrows.

"Small town thing, I guess." He shrugs. "The welcome wagon welcomes you to the neighborhood. Comes to your door, leaves menus for restaurants and all the news about the town." His gaze falls down my body one more time. A smirk forms as he checks out my heels. "You don't seem from around here, so I can show you a real Alaskan man."

"Then you're the last person who should welcome her to town." The guy from outside claps Jed on the shoulder. "He's really just an Arizona boy pretending to play an outdoorsman."

I laugh, and Jed stares at me as though he can't believe I make that sound.

"Meet Cade... Greene," Jed says, and Cade puts his hand over the table between us.

I shake it, and a spark runs up my arm. He smiles and the air rushes from my lungs. This is how I'm used to feeling when a gorgeous man approaches me. I glance at Jed for a moment, wondering why I didn't get that feeling with him.

"So you're brothers?" I ask.

They both shake their heads. "Step."

That explains how different they look. Cade's hair is longer, darker, and wavy, and he has a lot more scruff. The type of scruff you want to feel between your thighs.

"Cool." I sip my beer.

Cade shakes his head and grabs an empty glass from the stack in the middle of the table and pours a beer from the other pitcher. "Trust me, you'll like this one more." He leans past Jed and places it in front of me.

Jed sighs. "She already has the best beer we sell."

"So you guys make the beer, I take it?" I arch an eyebrow.

They look at one another and back at me.

"We own the brewery," Cade says.

I look around the place some more, thankful no one is paying me much attention anymore. The brewery suits them. Big silver barrels behind glass on one side, the tables are all dark wood and bulky with oversized chairs. Televisions arranged in a line above the bar showcase an array of sports, and there's a big sign made out of steel that says Truth or Dare Brewery prominently displayed so it's the first thing you see when you walk in.

"Very nice. I'm not much of a beer drinker, so I'm probably not a good judge."

Jed pushes Cade's closer as though he welcomes the competition. "Just take a sip and tell Cade you like mine better."

I'm sure that grin paired with his wink gets Jed a lot of places, like between a woman's legs.

"We earn money from both, so it's not a real competition," Cade says and rocks back on his heels. His body language says the complete opposite of what his lips did.

I sip Cade's beer and swallow. They say nothing, waiting for me to speak. "It's good. They're both good."

"If you had to finish a glass, which would you choose?"

"Um..." I'd rather be judging their beers than explaining who I am, so I play along and hope that as it winds down, I'll be able to speak with Clara alone. "I guess I like the lighter one."

"Cade's?" Jed asks with distaste.

I shrug. "I told you I'm not really a beer drinker."

"Hold up." Jed leaves the stool and Cade takes his spot.

Suddenly I feel like the stuffed animal caught in a game of tug-of-war.

"He's going to bring you his peach-flavored beer from this summer. It was our best seller last year and he likes to brag about it." He glances at my plate that I've abandoned. "Do you not like the food?"

"Oh no, I'm just not as hungry as I thought."

Cade nods. "Did you know Mrs. Harrison?"

Think fast, Presley. "Not very well, but I read her obituary and wanted to pay my respects." I want to pat myself on the back. "Presley." I put out my hand.

"Good to meet you, Presley. Sorry about the whole scene when you walked in, but no one is shy to let you know you're an outsider in this town."

I smile and sip his beer for something to do. A grin lights

up his face as if it makes his day that I chose his beer to drink.

"I almost didn't come. Felt it wasn't my place."

He pours himself a glass of Jed's beer and I tilt my head but don't ask. "I think if she touched your life in some way, it's your place to be here. Have you spoken to Clara?"

Cade shifts his weight to get up, but in a panic, I place my hand on his thigh to stop him, retracting it quickly when the heat from his leg seeps into my fingertips. "Not yet. She looked very distraught when I came in and saw her with her husband by her side."

He laughs. "Not her husband. That's her best friend, Xavier, also my brother."

My throat closes for a moment. "Oh, so you're close to Clara?"

He drinks his beer. "I've known her since she was born."

I nod. "And her dad? Is he still alive?"

His lips tip down, so I know the answer before he opens his mouth. "No. Unfortunately, his fishing boat went missing during a storm a little more than five years ago. He and some other men from Sunrise Bay died."

I clear my throat. "So it's just Clara then?"

He nods as though he can understand the pain she must be inflicted with. "Yeah, but she and Xavier are super close. That's my stepmom next to her. She'll make sure Clara gets through this."

"That's good. I'm sure that would make her mom happy."

He studies me for a second. "God, you look really familiar."

I can understand why, and I'm surprised that no one immediately saw the resemblance when I walked in. To me it's there, but maybe because I know what I look like as a brunette versus the dyed blonde hair I've had for years.

"I don't think we've ever met," I say.

Jed walks back over, a welcome interruption to our conversation that was hitting a little close to home. I promised myself that when I arrived in town, I would go to the source. I would go right to Clara and tell her before anyone figured it out. Now I can't help but feel as if there's a ticking clock hovering over my head.

Coming here was a mistake. All I wanted was to hear some happy stories about Clara's mom, to understand what kind of woman she was.

"Here you go," Jed says. "This is the best one. It's—"

"Peach?" I finish for him.

He turns to Cade with narrowed eyes. "Regardless of sour grapes here, it's the best flavor we've done."

"Jed!" a blonde across the room hollers.

Jed places the beer down in front of me. "I'll be back, let me know what you think." He rushes off.

I slide the beer closer to Cade. "I'm not sure I can drink any more beer. It's really not my drink."

He's quick to stand. "Let me get you something else. We have some cider. Or I can make you a mixed drink."

"I'm fine, really." I slide off the stool. "I should get going anyway."

He stands as well, and that's when I realize that we're way too close. "I can get Clara—"

"No. No. Leave her be. Thank you for keeping me company, and please thank your brother for me too."

"Do you need a ride or anything?" Cade asks.

I shake my head. "No. Thanks though."

I step around him without waiting for him to say goodbye. When I pass Clara, her gaze flickers up and our eyes lock for a moment, making me pause. The Xavier guy I thought was her husband comes over and says something to Clara, tearing her gaze away from mine.

I'd love to go over and whisper in her ear, "You're not alone."

Instead, I walk out the door and onto the street of a town that should have been my home.

Chapter Three

"Okay then, let's talk about the blonde."
~ Jed Greene

Cade

"Let me guess—you scared her away?" Jed comes to my side as I stare at the blonde walking out of the brewery. She pauses near Clara and almost looks as though she's going to say something, but then she continues on.

Nikki steps between us. "You know, they say funerals bring out the dark secrets of people's pasts."

I raise my hand, not wanting to hear Nikki's crap right now.

"Well your next segment is walking down the street right now," Jed says. He picks up the glasses. "There's obviously something wrong with her."

"Why? Did she give any clues as to who she is?" Nikki asks.

"No, she was more into Cade than me." Jed shakes his head. "Like I said, definitely something wrong."

I scoff and push his shoulder. "You know I have more game than you."

"Game? You don't even have a man on the board."

My brother Adam walks into the brewery, dressed in his forest ranger uniform, and stops at Clara, hugging her and offering his condolences. I'm sure most of the room is watching him carefully because we're all still confused as to why Adam's wife left him two weeks ago. He married too young. I told him that back when he was marrying his high school sweetheart. So maybe it's not that big of a surprise that she up and left without a reason. At least not one he's sharing with us.

My sister Chevelle heads our direction with concern on her face. "He's got bags under his eyes," she whispers because she wants me to fix it.

Another eldest son responsibility. I fix everything for Chevelle, but that's because she's my youngest sibling and has had a rough go of it since my mom died.

"I know, but he'll get through it. He'll move on," I say.

The four of us stand there, watching our brother hug Clara, both of them looking on the verge of tears.

"We should do something to cheer him up," Nikki says.

"How about a game night?" Chevelle asks. "He always loves card games."

"I say the guys do a run to the strip club in Anchorage," Jed says.

Nikki smacks him on the back of the head.

Adam separates from Clara and looks around the room. We all turn around as if we weren't just talking about him. I collect dirty cups from some tables then carry the stack to the kitchen to get them washed, and on my way out, I find Clara in the hallway by the bathroom. Before I can say anything, she pushes the back door open and steps outside.

I glance down the hallway, not seeing Xavier, who's been at her side the entire day. Going back into the kitchen,

I grab a plate of our signature quesadillas that's just come off the grill and follow her.

She's sitting at a table we keep in back, separated from customer parking by a wall, for the employees when they're on break.

"Hey," I say, sliding in across from her and pushing the quesadillas toward her.

"Hi, Cade." She looks up. "Is someone looking for me?"

I shake my head. "I saw you sneak away."

She nods like she figured someone would. "I can't take the sad eyes anymore. I mean, it was expected. She was sick."

"It doesn't make it any less hard." I pull apart the quesadilla. Hopefully, if she sees the gooey cheese, she'll be enticed to eat something.

"I think it's more because I'm the last one. I have no more family."

I squeeze her forearm. "You have us, the Greenes. You know that."

She nods again as though she understands what I'm saying. Maybe I'd be better off to leave her alone.

"There's so much to do. Her house needs to be emptied. And the store." Clara shakes her head. "I mean, I have time when I'm not working at the library, but it's all so daunting. I have to go to Trent Lawson's office tomorrow to go over the will. It's just a lot."

"If you need help, we're here. I can help with the store or help move some stuff from the house. Whatever you need. Xavier will be here for a few weeks since the season is over and tourist season isn't for another two months. We'll get it all handled."

She stands and heads over to the store beside the brewery, digging the keys out of her pocket. She opens the back door. There are cobwebs and dust on the door because no one has stepped foot in there in some time. She swivels the key off the chain and holds it out toward me. I stand and walk over to her then open my palm.

She places the key there. "I have no use for this. It's yours. I know you and Jed have been wanting to expand the brewery."

"Are you sure? We'll pay you of course." Her mom would've bought this storefront decades ago, so Clara will get a good profit by selling it to us.

We step inside, and she flicks on the lights. It smells musty, and it's obvious no one has been in here for a while, but when I look around, all I see is potential and profits for our business.

She picks up a spool of thread from one of the shelves. "We'll figure it out, but she would've wanted you guys to have it. What am I going to do with it? I can't thread a needle, let alone teach someone to sew."

"Thanks, but it doesn't seem right that we're talking about it today."

She smiles at me. "Maybe, but when then? I couldn't be in that bar with all those people staring at me for any longer. Xavier's all over me like a damn linebacker. I appreciate it, I do, but I just want to be by myself. Handle her affairs, remember her, and move on."

I hug her. I was exactly where she was years ago. "I know it hurts and you want to move on and forget this pain, but believe me, one day you'll think of her and it won't hurt nearly as much."

She squeezes me. "Thank you for that."

I nod.

"There you are." Xavier walks in, stepping over patterns and fabric that must have fallen at some point.

Clara smirks. "I'm here. Can you just take me home?"

Xavier nods and puts his arm around her. "Yeah. Let's go."

"Thanks, Clara," I say.

She turns around. "You're welcome."

Xavier is babying her because we know what it's like to lose a parent. Clara's lost two and her grandma. As annoying as my big family can be at times, I can't imagine having no one left.

As I'm about to pocket the key and keep this conversation to myself until I know she means it and wants to sell it to us, Jed walks through the door. "So is it true?"

"What?"

"That she gave you the key? That she's going to sell us the space?"

So much for keeping it quiet and making sure it's not just her grief talking.

———

I LOOK AROUND THE SPACE, trying to figure how much we'll have to renovate, how we'll manage the support beams by tearing down the wall.

Jed's already got a pencil and an old pattern laid out, writing a floor plan on the back of it. "Do you think we need more seating? Maybe we should just expand our production so we can offer more flavors, more options for grocery stores."

"I think we should expand the seating. Remember during tourist season how long the line was? We had to turn people away. Doubtful we could get a beer garden in here, but it might be worth talking to an architect."

"Then we'd have to go to the town and get approval.

Plus, we're in Alaska. We'd only be able to use it less than half the year."

"You make Alaskans sound weak. We're used to braving the cold." I walk to the front window and the foggy glass that Mrs. Harrison used to keep crystal clear. "This seems horribly disrespectful. Let's wait to make plans until Clara has a few days to think this through."

He drops the pencil and crosses his arms. Jed isn't an asshole—he's become my best friend over the years, which is funny since I hated him when he first came to town—but sometimes he gets tunnel vision and forgets his manners.

So I'm not surprised that after a moment he nods, agreeing with me. "Okay then, let's talk about the blonde."

"I don't really care who she is."

He jumps off the table and meets me at the window. "I'm not saying you care in the same way Nikki does, but you couldn't stop looking at her."

"Funny that you think I was into her, yet you went and tried to snatch her up first."

He laughs and stuffs his hands into his jeans pockets. "Why do you think I did that?"

I glance at him. "Because she was more into me, you're gonna act like you hit on her to spur me to make a move? Of course you'd play it that way."

He chuckles again and holds up his hands. "I swear. I have no interest in the woman."

I shake my head. "Yeah, okay."

"She didn't give off the vibe I like." He shrugs.

"Vibe?"

"She looks like the kind of girl who has a stipulation of, like, four dates before she'll sleep with you." He smacks me on the back. "That's more you than me."

I tilt my head and wrinkle my forehead. "And what exactly does that say about me?"

"Come on, you were the steady boyfriend in high school. Reese?"

"I'm far from the guy I was in high school."

"I'm amazed you got out of college without a fiancée." He walks back, snags the papers from the desk, folds them, and puts them in his back pocket.

"I wasn't looking for one. In fact, I purposely made sure not to go down that road."

He turns around and points at me. "Exactly, and that's the difference between us. I didn't have to mentally tell myself not to get serious with anyone. I knew I'd never get to that point with a woman."

I'm not going to call Jed out on his crap, but his parents' divorce kind of messed him up. His dad was a complete douche and cheated on Marla, then he apparently cheated on his second wife too. I think Jed is worried that adultery is a genetic affliction or something.

"Tell me one reason why you aren't married with two kids yet?" He crosses his arms and gives me a look like, "This should be good."

"First of all, I'm only thirty. And I'm not getting married, maybe ever." I brush past him toward the back door. I haven't made my mind up completely about whether I'll ever get married, but I'm damn sure not ready to open myself up for that anytime soon.

Jed stops before we exit and stares at me for a moment as though he wants to call me out, but he places his hand on my shoulder and doesn't go there. Instead he says, "A date doesn't mean forever. If you see the blonde again, ask her out."

I say nothing. Presley's and my conversation was easy. I

love that she knows nothing about me. She doesn't know I'm Cade Greene, once a twelve-year-old boy who lost his mother tragically. Cade Greene, son of handyman extraordinaire, Hank Greene, who took over the business from his dad. Cade Greene, stepson to Marla Greene, the woman involved in every fundraiser and committee in town. And Cade Greene, brother to four, stepbrother to four, and half brother to one. My family name in this town has a long past, and I never forget that. Neither does anyone in town.

I shrug. "Maybe if I ever see her again."

He opens the door, the low light flickering through the trees behind the back parking lot. "Thata guy!"

Of course, I'm sure that woman is long gone by now.

Chapter Four

"I thought I'd never see you again."
~ Cade Greene

Presley

The next morning, I take an Uber from Glacier Point Resort in Lake Starlight to the lawyer's office since I didn't want to stay in Sunrise Bay.

I climb out of the car under the dark awning that says Trent Lawson, Attorney at Law. The bell rings when I step into the small office. There's one desk with a middle-aged receptionist sitting behind it.

She peeks up and her eyes widen. I saw her at the funeral yesterday. She was among the group of people talking about whatever that competition thing was. "Hello," she says and looks down. "You must be Presley Knight?"

I nod.

She smiles. "Let me just poke my head in to see if Mr. Lawson is ready for you."

"Thank you." I give her a nervous smile.

She stands and heads down a short hallway, so I take a seat in the waiting room. I'd really hoped to talk to Clara before today. My stomach twists over how she'll react to the news that I'm in town. Then again, I'm just assuming she's been kept in the dark. Maybe her parents were up-front with her all these years.

"He'll see you now."

The receptionist waits for me to stand, then she walks me down the hall to his office door, holding her hand out for me to enter. After I do, she shuts the door.

I get my first look at Mr. Lawson, and my initial thought is that he doesn't suit his voice. He's a shorter male, stout and balding, but his voice holds this timbre that made me think he was six-five, two-twenty, and played rugby when he wasn't in a courtroom.

He called me five days ago to tell me he had a client who had passed away and my name was listed in the will. I knew immediately who had died, and I was surprised to hear that she even knew who I was to be in her will. I booked a flight to Alaska, much to my mom's dismay, and here I am—ready to get whatever broach or photo or letter of apology the deceased woman has left me. Then I'll go back to Connecticut and my parents, especially my mom, will be happy it's all over with.

Of course, there isn't a ton for me to go back to other than a few friends and my parents. I haven't really been hitting it out of the park in the job or social arena since graduation. Barely making rent, working jobs I don't enjoy but enable me to live on my own. I'm not even going to think about my barren love life.

"Miss Knight. Good to meet you," Mr. Lawson says as he stands behind his desk.

"Thank you, same." His office chairs are surprisingly comfortable, and I cross my legs, placing my purse on my lap.

"I called you in on your own because as you may have guessed, Clara does not know you exist."

I nod although I didn't know that for sure.

He pulls out an envelope from the file folder on his desk and hands it to me. My name is written on the outside in handwriting I don't recognize. "This is for you. She's written one to Clara as well. I advised her against her decision, but she was adamant that these were her last wishes."

I shake my head. "I'm not sure I understand."

"Your mo—Denise owned a building downtown. It was a sewing store, but she also taught lessons there or hosted group outings where she'd teach people how to complete a certain craft in one night. She was very talented with a needle and thread."

"Yes, I'm aware of her store. I went by yesterday and it looked pretty empty."

"With her being sick, Clara didn't have a lot of time..." He shakes his head. "Anyway, as you might not have known, your fath—Walter passed years back in an accident on a fishing vessel. That left only Clara and... well, you."

I nod, wishing he'd get to the point.

"Clara got the house, but when it came to the commercial building..."

"What is it?" I sit up straighter.

He sighs. "She left it to both you *and* Clara. The store, the building, is yours and hers to do with what you want. And if one of you wants to buy the other out, you can, or one of you can abandon the building, which would gift it to the other. You could both decide to sell it and split the profits. I tried to get an estimate of the value, but there are a lot of variables like whether you want to keep it as the sewing place or make it something else. I have all the appraisal paperwork in this folder for you to look over."

I hold up my hand. "Together?"

He sighs and nods.

"Is she crazy? Or was she?"

"I warned her I didn't think it was a viable plan. She didn't have enough money in her estate for Clara to buy you out. I'm not sure about your financial situation..."

I shake my head to say I don't have that kind of money. "There is so much wrong with this situation."

"My job is to tell my clients the risks and rewards of any situation, but this was her decision. Now, I'd like to plan a time for you and Clara to come in together. I'll be here when she's told, and I'll probably invite a close friend of hers in for support."

So he'll bring in someone for her, but I don't need a support system? Easy to see whose side this town is on. I hate when my mom's right.

I stand. "Okay. Just let me know." I round the chair toward the door.

I hear his chair slide back. "Miss Knight. I need to know if you're interested in the building?"

Turning around, I remember another piece of my mom's advice—keep your cards close to your chest because most people who normally wouldn't cheat will, given the opportunity. We might not be playing rummy right now, but he wants to know what cards I'm holding so he can help Clara because she's a Sunrise Bay townie. Well, if all I get is half a building for not being the chosen one, so be it, but I'll let him know once I meet Clara myself.

"Just let me know when you want me to meet her and we'll talk then." I open his door and leave his office.

INSTEAD OF REQUESTING AN UBER, I walk around Sunrise Bay. Spring in Alaska is very different from Connecticut. The ground back home is thawing already, with green buds on trees, whereas everything here is still dreary and gray. Part of me wonders what the bay looks like during tourist season.

I find a park bench and open the letter from Denise Harrison, who until right this moment was a woman I've hated, I've been curious about, and I've mourned well before her death.

PRESLEY,

WHAT A BEAUTIFUL NAME. I'm not sure I would've chosen it, but it's lovely. I'm sure you're wondering why I'm deciding to write my first letter to you when you're twenty-nine years old and I'm on my deathbed. But I feel that I need to try to make amends and help you understand before I take my last breath. I know about my mother, Beatrice's letters and gifts to you. It was very kind of your parents to allow her to do that for you. But when I gave you up, I understood my decision and that they were now your parents, as hard as that was for me. I do hope you realize we didn't come to our decision lightly. And I'm sure you're even more confused finding out about Clara, your biological sister who we kept.

Oh, Presley, I so wish I would've thought life could change, but when we became pregnant with you, we were two poor kids trying to make it, and at the time, we just didn't think you'd have a decent shot at life if we raised you. We were in a bad place as a couple and well... good or bad, we gave you up so you'd have a wonderful life. A better life than the one we thought we could provide you.

After your grandma Beatrice died, I found the pictures your mom sent to her. It was the first time I learned of the correspondence you had with her. The woman always did amaze me with what she could get people to agree to. You've grown into a beautiful woman.

I guess I'll get to the point because if I were you, an old lady's dying apology after all these years wouldn't be worth much. I want to give you a chance and a reason to stay in Sunrise Bay. It's a wonderful little town and I hope you'll consider taking over the store, making it into whatever you want. But please do it with Clara. You two are the last in both your father's and my families, and I'd love nothing more than you two to be true sisters.

I know I'm asking a lot and I understand that you might just tear this letter up, sign off your rights to half the building, and go back to Connecticut. I'm sure I'd do that because sometimes I think I've lived scared my entire life. When I became pregnant with you, your father and I had run away from this small town and returned shortly after the adoption. I've tried to tell Clara as she grew older, but I could never bring myself to see what she would think of me after I told her. I'm a chicken. There you have it. You come from chicken genes. Well, not your father, he wasn't a chicken at all, but that resulted in his death.

I'm losing track now. I do hope you stay and give life here a shot, but I understand if you don't.

I can't change how you feel, but please know, there was never a morning I didn't wake up and you weren't in my thoughts. A constant reminder of your biggest regret is painful to live with. Please don't ever be like me. Don't live with the what-ifs—go find the answers.

. . .

LOVE,
   Denise Harrison

P.S. CLARA CAN BE hard to warm up. Give her a chance.

I DROP the letter in my lap, annoyed that I'm supposed to somehow cater to Clara's feelings. But as I read her line about the what-ifs, something resonated inside me. I already have enough what-ifs in my life. What if I would have majored in English rather than business? I might be happier. What if I would've stayed with Lincoln? I could be married right now. What if I hadn't been given up for adoption? I look around. This could have been my town. I would've just lost the woman who raised me.

There's nothing promising for me in Connecticut, but staying in Sunrise Bay and opening a business with a sister who didn't even know I existed until today? I'd have to be crazy to consider it.

I stuff the letter in my purse and walk back to Sunrise Bay's small downtown area. I head past the brewery to the sewing storefront. It's small but nestled between a brewery and a butcher. The town is cute, like something you'd see in those cheesy Christmas movies where singers carol down the streets, everyone knows everyone, and people have your back. Is that such a bad place to live?

"You again." Cade walks out of the brewery. He's putting on a jacket over his dark plaid shirt. He really is sexy. "I thought I'd never see you again."

I have to admit, for whatever reason, I feel as if Cade could be another "what if" should I decide to leave.

"Here I am," I say, holding my arms out to my sides as though I'm inviting him to look at me.

And he does look his fill while I try not to let my entire body shiver under his attention. Then he looks back at the brewery before giving me his full attention. "Are you free for dinner tonight?"

I blink a couple of times. "Dinner?"

"Yeah, you name the place. I can give you a few references who will vouch for me not being a creep or an asshole."

I giggle. It's been a long time since I've laughed and that's saying something. "Sure. I'm staying in Lake Starlight. Glacier Point Resort?"

His head rears back a bit as though I've surprised him. Glacier Point is fancy, but it's not my money, it's my parents'. "Perfect. There's a restaurant in town there called Terra and Mare. I'll call and make a reservation."

"Great." After a bit of awkward silence, I speak again. "I guess we should exchange phone numbers then."

We pull out our phones and enter our information in the other's.

"I'll text you as soon as I know what time." He walks backward toward the brewery.

"Sounds good. Look forward to hearing from you."

"I can't wait." He smiles one more time and dips back into the brewery.

A loud "woohoo" echoes into the street from the brewery, and I feel a blush rush up to my cheeks. Is it really this easy to get a date here? Maybe what they say about Alaska having all the men is true.

Chapter Five

"This is like something from a TV show."
- Xavier Greene

Cade

"Way to go, man." Jed slaps me on the back and lets out a howl so loud I'm sure Presley heard him outside.

I can't stop smiling because she was so quick to accept my offer for dinner. "I gotta call Terra and Mare."

"Oh, you're not skimping, huh?" Jed says as I head over to the other side of the bar.

"Not everyone takes their dates to a food truck," Molly jokes.

I laugh while I listen to the phone ring. Someone answers, then puts me on hold.

"I've never gotten any complaints," Jed says, drawing a sketch of what he wants to do with the space next door. Looks like it's to scale this time. He's truly talented, and I always wonder why he came back here after college and isn't designing high-rises somewhere.

"Who said anything about complaints? I mean, a meal takes up a lot of time when you could be doing other things." She winks.

Jed laughs and glances my way. I slide my finger over my throat. Molly is way too flirtatious, and I already told Jed when she was hired on part-time that he couldn't egg on her antics like he has all the years she's been Nikki's best friend. He clears his throat and concentrates back on the drawing.

The doors open and Xavier walks in with Clara. Gone is the heartbroken girl I last saw. Now she looks pissed as she stalks up to the bar. Xavier looks at Jed and me with a cringe. I know she was talking to the lawyer today.

"Give me the hardest stuff you have." Clara slams her purse on the bar.

Molly's gaze shoots up, but she grabs a bottle of whiskey and pours her a shot glass. Clara downs it, her brown hair thrown up in a ponytail, and slams the glass down.

"Do not tell Nikki anything about this," Xavier whispers.

Like I would. I don't agree with her morning radio show shit.

Since we just opened, they're the only ones in here, so whatever is going on will only be between us.

"Don't tell her that the town librarian is getting plastered this early in the day?" Jed asks.

"Turns out Clara isn't the only Harrison left," Xavier says in a quiet voice.

My eyebrows come together. "What?"

Xavier nods and his eyes widen in an "I'm just as shocked as you but trying to be a good friend and not tell her how fucked-up this is" look. "The blonde. She's her sister."

My phone slips from my hand, dropping on the bar then down to the floor, cracking my screen. "Fuck!"

"That's why she looked familiar. I wondered if I'd banged her," Jed says.

We both shake our heads at him.

"Good for you that's not true." Jed smacks me on the back with a grin.

"Why's that good for Cade?" Xavier asks.

"He has a date with her tonight." Jed sounds like a proud father and I want to punch him for it.

"With who?" Xavier asks, not getting it.

"Presley," I say.

"The blonde," Jed chimes in.

"Oh, and Cade..." Clara raises her hand. "I'm going to need that key back." She pushes the empty shot glass toward Molly, who refills it.

"What's she talking about?" I ask Xavier.

Jed's mood deflates faster than a carnival blow-up toy when you get it home. "The space next door?"

"Mrs. Harrison willed it to Clara *and* her sister," Xavier says.

My head falls back and Jed's fist slams on the bar top.

"What kind of mother does this?" Clara asks.

Xavier holds up his finger to us, whispering in her ear.

She shoves him. "I don't care. Isn't there bartender-client confidentiality?" she asks Molly. "You can't tell Nikki."

Molly shrugs and nods. Clara doesn't hold back, clearly the two shots already in her bloodstream.

"The mystery blonde? My sister. Half-sister, you think?" Clara shakes her head. "Did my mom get pregnant by some guy when she was a teenager?" Clara shakes her head again. "Did my dad have an affair?" Clara shakes her head. "She's my full sister. Half my mom. Half my dad. My full outright sister." She pushes her glass to Molly.

Molly looks at us and Jed shakes his head.

"I mean, what kind of mother wouldn't tell me that?"

Xavier whispers something else in Clara's ear and her arms flail as if he's a fly she can't swat. He says to us, "They either run the store together, or one of them can buy the other out, or they can sell it altogether."

That explains why I've seen Presley in front of the window twice. And also why she looks so familiar. I realize now that she's basically Clara's twin but with dyed blonde hair, and a few years older. How the hell didn't I put two and two together before this?

"Wait," I say to Xavier, a memory sparking of ten years ago when Clara's grandma died. "Remember when her grandma died, and I told you I thought I saw Clara at the cemetery when I went to see mom? But I called her name, and she just ignored me..."

"It was her!" Xavier snaps his fingers and points.

They looked the same, and I thought it was Clara, but it was her—Presley.

"Damn, it must have been her." Xavier shakes his head. "Crazy. This is like something from a TV show. Who keeps a child a secret?"

I think he'd be surprised by how many skeletons people have in their closets. Being a pro-athlete, you'd think he'd know, since most of their dark secrets come out during their playing years. People want to pull celebrities down from their pedestals.

"And now ten years later, you're going on a date with her," Jed says.

"I'm not sure I can now. Seems unfair to Clara until this whole thing is cleared up."

Not to mention, I don't want Presley to find out I want the building too. She'll think the worst of me and where would that get us? Plus, she's obviously from way out of town, which means she's not staying in Sunrise Bay long-term unless she decides to do something with the building.

"How do I face her tomorrow?" Clara cries. "'Hey, I'm the daughter they kept. Want to braid each other's hair?'"

Clara's voice grows louder, so I tell Molly to give her one more. She deserves it.

WHEN I GET BACK to my house after getting the screen fixed on my phone, I debate whether I should go on the date with Presley. Terra and Mare had no reservation available anyway, but we could eat at the restaurant in Glacier Point. But I can't help but think it's weird now that I know *who* she is.

Sitting on the couch, I stare at my phone as though I'm waiting for a call, but really I'm trying to force myself to make one.

Jed walks in and stops in his tracks. "Stop being a dumb-ass. You know she's not going to stay in town."

"And if she does?"

"Then you can continue seeing her if you want." His footsteps barrel up the stairs.

We live in the house I grew up in—me, Jed, Fisher, and now Adam since he and Lucy split. The girls share a house closer to our parents. Nikki was staying with us when she first moved back from college but said she didn't like being by herself in the apartment and she didn't want to move into the house with all us guys.

I sink back into the couch, pissed that after all these years, I find a woman I want to date and she turns out to be Sunrise Bay's secret love child. The gossip brigade will eat this up. If she dates me, it would only make it worse for her.

I hammer out a text before I change my mind.

Me: *So sorry, something came up. Rain check?*

The three dots appear immediately.

Presley: *Sure. Not sure how long I'll be in town but let me know when you're available.*

Me: *Definitely. I'll message you tomorrow.*

That gives me twenty-four hours. She might be gone by tomorrow evening anyway. Xavier said she and Clara are meeting in the morning.

Jed comes trudging back down the stairs. "God, I'm so pissed. That building was ours. I could see perfectly what we could do in there. I think we might have to look at relocating or opening up a second location." He sits down and places his remote for the Xbox in his lap, holding the one sitting on the coffee table out to me. The guy hides his remote because he thinks it's bad luck if any of the rest of us use it.

I blow out a breath, but what else do I have tonight now that I canceled my date?

"Could've gotten laid and now your sorry ass has to play video games with your brother." He clucks his tongue.

"I don't know about a second location. That's a huge expense. So is relocating."

He turns on the game console, and we wait for the game to load. "Then we have to convince that girl to give the building to Clara so that she'll give it to us."

I disregard him, knowing he's talking out of his ass like usual. My mind shifts to Presley while the game logo displays on the screen. "Can you imagine finding out your parents put you up for adoption and they kept their second born? Talk about fucking you up in the head."

Jed elbows me. "And you thought we had it bad."

Headlights light up the driveway, and Jed and I look at one another. Standing, we see who it is. I consider flipping the locks, but my dad will just remind us how it's still his house and we pay him rent to live here.

My dad, Hank, opens the front door and comes walking in with my ten-year-old half brother, Rylan.

"Hey, Ryguy," Jed says.

Rylan comes over and sits on the couch.

Marla walks in a few seconds later, a stack of our mail in her hands. "Come on, boys." She drops it on the table.

"To what do we owe this honor?" I ask since Rylan took over my remote for the game.

"Your brother wanted to spend the night." My dad tosses Rylan's soccer bag in the corner. "Can you take him to soccer in the morning?"

"And you two?" I ask, not really wanting to know.

"We're going on a date night." My dad slaps Marla's ass, and I gag. "Grow up." He shakes his head at me. "I heard you guys aren't getting Denise's shop after all, huh?"

I shake my head. "How'd you hear that?"

Marla walks around the living room, picking up things, then disappears into the kitchen. I swear it's Adam who's leaving the mess, but if I tell that to Marla or Dad, they'll tell us we should be doing everything we can for him, that he's going through a hard time.

"How do you think? Everyone knows. The gossip brigade." Marla comes back in with a garbage bag, tossing everything she views as trash.

Jed and Rylan continue to play, shifting left and right to see the screen whenever Marla gets in their line of vision.

"The gossip brigade." Jed laughs. "Shouldn't they be thankful they survived the war and just live in peace?"

The gossip brigade is a small group of military veterans who think they have the investigative skills to get any information they want. I'm fairly sure they're Nikki's primary source for her little radio station stunt.

"You know your sister will be announcing the news tomorrow morning," my dad says.

That makes my stomach sour. First, I cancel on the woman, and now before she and Clara can even meet, people in town will know who Presley is and the circumstances for her arrival in Sunrise Bay. At least anyone who hasn't already run into the gossip brigade. But since they mostly hang out in the Handyman Haven store, it explains how my dad found out.

"Okay, we're out. Call us if you have any problems. If we don't answer, don't worry, we'll call you back." Dad winks, and I suppress a full-body shiver. "Marla, it's their mess. For heaven's sake, stop."

Dad and Marla say their goodbyes and leave. I walk over behind the couch and ruffle Rylan's hair. I don't mind the kid spending the night. He trains for soccer so much that I don't see him as much as I should.

"How's Calista?" Jed elbows him.

"Stop it. She's annoying," he says, but there's a flush to his cheeks that makes me smile.

"You can't stop the Greene genes, kid. Women love us," Jed says, his thumbs flying over the controller.

"I'll order pizza." I go into the kitchen and pull out my phone. Before I order our dinner, there's something else I need to take care of.

Me: *Do me a favor and hold the story for one more day.*

The three dots come up.

Nikki: *Why?*

Me: *Put yourself in her shoes.*

Nikki: *Tell me the REAL reason and I'll consider it.*

Me: *What do you want me to say?*

Nikki: *I heard you asked her out. Come on big brother. Fess up.*

I blow out a breath, knowing exactly what she wants.

Me: *I like her. Is that what you want to hear?*

Nikki: *One day. Then it's my job to report what's going on. Make it count. ;)*

Me: *Thanks.*

Nikki: ☺ *who's your favorite sister?*

Me: *Chevelle*

Nikki: *Okay who's your favorite stepsister and think carefully about this...*

I laugh.

Me: *You of course.*

Nikki: *Good answer.*

I pocket the phone, happy she's willing to hold off. But still, I only saved Presley for twenty-four hours. Then we'll see if she can handle some of what comes with a small town. I'm not sure if I want her to handle it or run back home.

Chapter Six

"You're a reminder of the secrets people hide in their closets."
~ Mrs. Knight

Presley

I might as well get the Uber driver's personal number because every day, the same driver picks me up. I guess the area is small, but he's on autopilot when he drops me off at Trent Lawson's office the next morning.

Mr. Lawson's receptionist takes in my outfit. After Cade asked me out, I went shopping in downtown Lake Starlight, finding a new outfit at a boutique store for our date. I'm not letting it go to waste, even if my heels are a little fancy to meet a lawyer.

"Mr. Lawson," I say as if we're in such a big city she wouldn't remember me from yesterday or that Mr. Lawson isn't probably the only lawyer in this office.

"Nice to see you, Miss Knight. Please allow me to introduce myself this time." She puts out her hand. "I'm Beth Lawson."

I nod. She's his wife. So that whole lawyer-client privilege probably doesn't hold up. I shake her hand. "Nice to meet you, Mrs. Lawson."

"Please call me Beth."

"Okay, then call me Presley."

"You seemed... deep in thought last time, otherwise I would've introduced myself then."

I give her a wane smile.

She smiles back. "It's a very pretty name. Your mo—Denise was a good friend of mine." I'm not sure what look I give her, but she's quick to wave her hand. "She never told me about you or anything. It wasn't until she got sick and planned some things out with Trent that she divulged the information to me. I'm sure you have some personal feelings about it all, but I just wanted to let you know, she was a good person."

I'm stiff and robotic in my response. "Thank you." I'm not sure if that's the answer she wants to hear or not, but that's the one she's getting.

"Let's get you into Trent's office." She ushers me back but doesn't shut the door because someone else is joining us this time.

My stomach twists with the thought of coming face-to-face with Clara.

"Good morning, Miss Knight," Trent says, and I shake his hand, sitting down. "Have you come to a decision?"

What's with this guy? "No."

He nods and holds up his hands as if it's none of his business. But he's the one trying to push me into a decision. I hate lawyers.

Then I hear Beth talking to someone in the reception area. "Clara dear, how are you holding up?"

All I hear after that are murmurs. Trent looks at me as though he's trying to decipher how it makes me feel. Last I checked, this was a lawyer's office, not a psychologist's.

"Clara's here, Trent," Beth says behind me.

I close my eyes for a second before Clara comes into my peripheral view. It's not as if I haven't seen her, but now we're actually going to speak to one another. Do our voices sound similar?

"Hello, Clara, did Xavier come with you?" Mr. Lawson asks.

She sits in the chair next to me, and I brace myself to face her. Her eyes aren't red-rimmed like they were before. She's more casually dressed this time, wearing jeans, a sweater, and boots. Because she's an Alaskan and this is her hometown. Another stark reminder I was not raised here.

"No. I'm here by myself," Clara says.

"As you know, Clara, this is Presley. Presley, this is Clara."

The two of us look at one another, saying hello as if we're nine and our parents are at our sides, forcing us to be nice to one another.

At least we're on the same page. I can't imagine how I'd react if she was excited to discover she had a sister and wanted to be my best friend or something.

"So the building. You've both had a chance to think about it. Have either of you come to a decision?"

Why is this guy in such a rush to have us settle this?

"I haven't," I say.

"Me either."

He sets down an envelope labeled keys. "Okay. I want to make you aware of a call I received this morning. There's a third party interested in the property. They'd be willing to purchase it from you, then you'd split the money." He thumbs through some paperwork in front of him.

Clara glances at me from the corner of her eye. It's one of her friends, probably. A native Sunrise Bayer who can't bear to see the girl be tortured into handling this complicated situation herself, no doubt.

"I'm fine with that," Clara says.

"We don't even know for certain what the building is worth," I interject.

Clara huffs, but I ignore her.

Mr. Lawson nods. "I'm sure you looked over the paperwork I gave you yesterday. The appraisal came in at a hundred fifty thousand. The third party is offering a fair amount of a hundred twenty-five thousand. They'll take it as-is, so the two of you don't have to worry about anything. Other than a lot of papers pushing around, which you could do from Connecticut," he says to me. "And Clara, I know you aren't interested in the building."

"Yeah, I'm good with the sale," she says again.

"I hate to be the stop sign here, but how do we even know if it's a fair offer? Someone might offer us more on the open market. Plus, what if I want to keep it?"

Clara whips her head in my direction. "You can't be serious."

I turn toward her, and I'm struck by how similar we look now that I'm this close to her. Yeah, her hair is dark brown, the color mine used to be before I began dying it blonde. But our skin tone is the same, as are our lips. Having someone share the same characteristics with me after growing up with *no one* sharing any feels weird.

"I am serious," I say.

"You want to stay in Sunrise Bay? Is this because of Cade Greene? Because you're wasting your time if you think you're going to ride off into the sunset with him."

I throw my hands in the air. "What are you talking about? And how do you know about anything to do with me and Cade Greene?"

I'm used to gossip. Hell, I grew up in high society where the gossip isn't just that someone asked someone else out. It's that her dad embezzled from the company, or her dad is sleeping with his mom, or the business isn't going well and they're going to lose everything. And most of those are shitty lies made up to hurt someone.

"Isn't that the whole reason you've been showing up around town? To ignite rumors?"

I stand, unable to sit next to her anymore. "Ignite rumors? If you're going to be mad at someone, be mad at your mother. She didn't have to drag me back here, then write some letter about how she wants me to have a relationship with you. I think you have enough people in this town who have your back."

Clara flies up from her chair. "And they should. I'm from here. I was raised here."

"Well, I don't want to be here anyway." I grab the envelope on the desk with the keys to the store. I rip it open and take out one. "But this is mine. And you don't have a say on whether or not I accept an offer for the building."

"Oh please. What are you going to do? Open up a high heels shoe store? Because this is Alaska and I hate to break it to you, but you're going to fail."

I groan, open the door, and walk right by that Xavier guy waiting in the reception area for his darling Clara.

"Presley," Beth says.

But I fly out the door, heading right to the store as if I'm going to squat there and prevent anyone from buying it. I'm fully aware that I'm allowing my damn stubborn side to take over, but right now, I can't find it in myself to care.

THE BELL ATTACHED to the door rings as I step into the space. It's dirty, dusty, and cluttered. Three rows of sewing machines sit on tables, and the walls are filled with spools of thread, bins of rolled-up fabric under them. Books of patterns are stacked on a table in the corner.

Sitting in one of the chairs, I dial up my mom, happy that with the time difference, it's later in the morning there.

"Presley," she says. "What did the lawyer say?"

I called Mom last night after Cade canceled and I bought a new outfit. Not that Mom wouldn't have called me —the woman probably has a tracker embedded in me some-where. My mom takes the word overprotective as a compliment.

"There's a third party who wants to purchase the building."

She lets out a long, relieved breath. Just like she did when I told her I'd broken up with Lincoln after college. He wasn't the kind of man she envisions me marrying. FYI, that imaginary person lives in Connecticut and had the same upbringing I did—country club, private schools, and familial wealth. "Oh, thank heavens. Have you booked your flight home then?"

"No, I don't know what I'm going to do. It seems weird to me that I'm left this building and now someone wants to buy it from me. Plus, I'm expected to just take some offer instead of seeing what it can get on the open market?"

"How much did they offer?" she asks.

"One hundred twenty-five thousand."

"For a building in Smalltown, Alaska? Take it, Presley."

I look around the small building and can admit to myself that I'm amazed someone would even offer that. I spot the same handwriting that was in my letter scribbled on patterns splayed out on the tables. The woman who grew me in her belly, the one I share DNA with, spent the majority of her time here.

"My God, you're thinking about staying, aren't you?" From her tone, you'd think I told her I preferred cotton over cashmere.

"No. I don't know."

"Presley, think about this. That town doesn't want you. You're a reminder of the secrets people hide in their closets."

In Connecticut, no one would ever have told a soul about the child they gave up for adoption. Image is everything. So why is something drawing me to this place?

I say, "I haven't decided. I just think that if I sell, I should get fair value."

"Just take it and come home. You're not going to find what you're looking for there."

"And what do you think I'm looking for?"

She blows out a breath. "I'm sure you're curious as to who she was. When I adopted you, I wasn't naïve enough to think you'd never want to meet her. But she's passed on now. I'm afraid maybe her wanting you to take over this building is more for her other daughter than you."

I lean my head into my palm, stretching out on the table. There's no denying my mom has a point. But I feel freedom here. I'm not being pushed into the box my mom wants me in. This is somewhere I could spread my wings, for lack of a better term. Find out what *I* want in life, what I'm made of. And I'm not sure I can do that in Connecticut.

"Presley," my mom says, "I'll catch the first flight I can get. Help you navigate this and bring you home."

It's tempting, knowing that the people in this town might not want me here. Everything my mom is saying could very well be true.

I stand and go to the back of the building. There's a desk there, set away from the rest of the store. From the calculator and bills on top, I'd say this is where she did the business side of things. I sit down and open the drawers, finding journals of sketches she designed in most of them. I open the last drawer and pick up a journal.

I allow Mom to carry on while I continue to be nosy. "I can fix this for you. Or you can come home and your father…"

A picture slides out of the journal and I catch it before it falls to the floor. It's the same picture my mom showed me when she told me they adopted me—a typical newborn picture taken in the hospital and it's of me. There's no name on the back, but I know it's me just the same. I scour the pages of the journal, hoping it was hers from when she gave me up and she anguished about whether she was making the right decision. Sadly, it's just business plans.

The bell chimes and I stand, rounding the partition to the front of the store. My mom continues telling me all the options that involve me leaving this town and returning back to her.

"I gotta go, Mom," I say.

"Presley."

I click to end the call and look at the woman standing across the room, wondering what she wants to yell at me about now.

"Can we talk?" Clara asks like a scorned puppy with her tail between her legs.

Let's hope this goes better than the first time.

Chapter Seven

"I'm not looking for a prince to swoop in."
- Presley Knight

Cade

After I drop Rylan at soccer, I head over to the brewery because this is my life. I'm either working or doing things with my family. Plus, the twenty-four-hour deadline I have from Nikki is on my mind.

Speaking of which, I'm listening to her now to make sure she's abiding by her word.

"The buzz around Sunrise Bay is which two companies will be named this month to collaborate on duo night. After last month's collaboration between Mary from Bakey Cakey and Chuck from Meatmarket, the next two participants will have their work cut out for them in planning a fun night for the community. Mary outdid herself with those tasty cakes that looked like beef."

Thankfully, my family are people of their words. I breathe a sigh of relief and turn off the station as I drive through downtown. It's quiet for a Saturday, and as I round the back of the brewery and park, I look at Mrs. Harrison's space. Guilt weighs on me over Jed putting in that offer for the building, but when he woke me in the middle of the night with his crazy idea, it sounded like a good option. Clara doesn't want it, and I doubt Presley does either. Who would want to stick around a town where you're the spotlight of the gossip mill? And she would be if she stayed.

Walking into the brewery, I don't bother going to the front of the building, but stay in the office to get some paperwork done.

My phone rings in my pocket and I pull it out, seeing Jed's name on the screen. "What's up?"

"Xavier just called. I guess the offer for us to buy the building wasn't met well by your girl. Things went downhill between her and Clara from there."

I run my hand down my face and around my neck and pull to release all the stress. "So it's a no."

"I have a few tricks up my sleeve. Maybe we could figure out a way to make her want to leave."

"Jesus, Jed."

"Then the only other option is for us to go over there. Talk to her. Let her know it's us. That we're up-front, honest guys and the offer is a solid one."

"Or we just don't expand."

He laughs. "You don't know me at all, do you? I get it if you don't feel comfortable, since you want to bang her, but I'm going to head over there now."

"I think we should just let them—"

"I'll let you know how it goes."

Click.

Damn Jed. The guy doesn't have an off switch. Clara and Presley are dealing with a lot right now. We should give them time to sort it out.

I grab my coat and walk out of the front entrance of the brewery. Sure enough, Jed is already parked and rounding

Meatmarket, heading toward the old sewing store. He smacks on his charismatic smile. He probably practiced his speech on the way over.

"Let's do this." He smacks his hands together and rubs them.

"You're going to get your ass kicked." I open the door, allowing him to go into the sewing store first.

Clara and Presley are in there, looking as if they're in a standoff. Clara's at the front of the store and Presley's near the back. They both turn their attention our way.

"You need to give us a minute," Clara says, holding up her hand.

"Just let us plead our case," Jed says and walks by Clara, sliding up on a table between them as though he's going to play mediator.

"Case?" Presley asks.

"These are the buyers," Clara fills her in.

Presley's gaze shoots to mine and she huffs. "Convenient."

"I did an honest comparison, and the fair value is more like a hundred thirty thousand, so if you want us to go up that high, we'll do it, but I think the as-is clause has to be enticing, no?" Jed looks around. "We can get rid of all this junk."

"It's not junk," Clara says.

"Of course not, but what are you going to do with six sewing machines?" Jed's quick to change his approach. Seriously, I know he hates his father, but sometimes he's so much like him and he thinks he can sell anything to anybody.

"Maybe we're going to open the store back up." Presley shoots me a glare.

Shit. She's angry with me.

Jed laughs.

Bad move.

"Do you have something to say, Jed?" Clara asks.

He holds up his hands. "Well, if you two could actually thread a needle and sew two pieces of fabric together, then I wouldn't laugh, but clearly..." His eyes zero in on Presley's heels and roam up her outfit. She looks gorgeous. "Neither of you are into sewing your own clothes."

"You know nothing about me." Presley crosses her arms and juts out her hip. Her jeans are tight, showcasing the curve of her hips and calves, and I can't help but wonder what her legs would look like if I peeled those jeans down to the floor.

"I know you're wearing high heels with no socks and it's spring in Alaska. I know the jeans you're wearing are designer."

Strike that whole thing about him being like his father. Jed is not selling this.

"Let me intervene," I say, taking a seat at the table across from Jed.

"Oh please, what? Are you going to try to seduce me to get the space?" Presley asks.

This is what I was afraid of. "That's not what I was doing."

She nods as if she's got my number. "Really? Do you always ask out girls you just met?" She looks at Clara. "Is Cade here the Casanova of Sunrise Bay?"

Clara bites her lip. She knows I'm not like that, and telling the truth will only hurt my case. "No. He doesn't date a lot."

Fucking hell.

"You were different," I say, but Presley raises her hand.

"It doesn't matter. Obviously that whole situation is

over now. You tried to go behind my back and get the building from me."

My forehead wrinkles. "What?"

"I think you have it wrong," Jed says.

Presley waves her hands, reminding me of a child who puts her fingers in her ears and says no, no, no. She points at Jed and me. "Listen, I know you want the building. And I know you want to sell it," she says to Clara. "I don't know what I want yet, so just give me some space."

Jed hops off the table. He's not one to easily accept defeat. "This is a lot for you to take on. Not even just the store. Cleaning all this, making it your own, getting rid of whatever you want to sell. And then you have the town. The gossip mill around here is not easy to handle."

Presley's eyes narrow at Jed, so I hop down and go to his side. She turns her laser eyes on me.

"He means you should think about those things before committing," I say.

"Oh really? Please enlighten me."

"I saved you for twenty-four hours with our sister, Nikki. Well, my stepsister, but his real sister," I say as Jed shakes his head and Presley looks as though she couldn't care less. "She won't report this whole thing on her radio show, but tomorrow morning, the entire story about you being Mrs. Harrison's daughter will be on the news."

"You saved me?"

I run a hand through my hair. "Yeah, it's nothing. Don't worry about it."

She scowls. "Oh, I'm not worried about it. Do you people really think your small town gossip has anything on what I have going on back home? It can't be any worse than attending a private school with privileged youth. The conniving and the lies would make your head spin. So I don't need your saving, Cade."

Clara laughs, and I look back at her. She bites her lip to stop herself, but I can tell she's enjoying this.

Jed glances at me. "He's just trying to help."

"Oh my God. I'm not looking for a prince to swoop in. Why does everyone in my life think I need saving? I don't. I'm a grown woman."

My eyebrows rise. Is this the same sweet woman from yesterday?

"So what, you're going to stay in town?" Jed says it with a laugh on the edge of his tone. Even I know that's the wrong move.

"Maybe I am."

"You are?" Clara asks.

Jed and I part to allow the two sisters to look at one another.

"I don't know." Presley shrugs.

Clara doesn't say anything, and the room goes quiet.

"Can we talk?" Presley asks Clara in a calmer voice.

Clara nods and walks forward. "It's why I came here. Because I didn't like how I left it. That's not me. This is just a lot to deal with."

Jed and I share a look of surprise.

"I have no idea how to act," Presley says with a vulnerability that makes my heart squeeze.

"Come on. I'll show you around town," Clara says, then tosses me a key. "Lock up, boys."

I catch it, and they walk out, turning right down the street.

"What the fuck just happened?" Jed runs a hand through his hair. "This was ours. Your girl cannot be thinking she's going to stay and take over this place."

I'm still staring at the door. "Suffice it to say, she's not my girl. And probably never will be."

He smacks me on the back. "I think you dodged a bullet."

We walk out of the building and I lock the store. Jed walks over to the brewery while I stare down the street. There's this feeling in the pit of my stomach saying that there's still something there. Regardless of whether Presley's going to deny it, we have a connection. Maybe if she decides to stay in town and we don't get to expand Truth or Dare, it's not such a bad thing. Just don't tell Jed.

Chapter Eight

"Welcome to Sunrise Bay."
~ Ethel Greene

Presley

Clara puts on her mittens and I put on my hat that isn't nearly as wintery warm as hers. I'm not going to complain about my heels and the cold weather though, since that's opening myself up for more ridicule.

A group of four men sitting on a bench outside a store called the Handyman Haven stare at us as we walk past.

Clara tugs on the sleeve of my coat and nods. "Let's go toward the bay."

I follow her, and neither of us says anything for a long time.

"Do you really want the building?" she asks.

I shrug. "I'm still deciding. I'm still processing, to be honest."

She stops, and I do the same to see if she's okay. "Did you know?"

"Know that I was adopted?"

She nods.

"Yeah. Did you know about me?" I ask.

Her shoulders sink. "I knew nothing. Nothing at all. Mom mentioned in her letter that Grandma Beatrice was in contact with you?"

"Yeah, she sent me birthday cards and my mom sent her pictures."

She flops down on a bench as though she doesn't have the energy to continue our walk. My feet thank her. "I'm just in so much shock. I mean, how did they never tell me that I had a sister?"

"You'd know better than me. You were their daughter."

She looks over and I'm still struck by how similar we look, although she doesn't wear the makeup I do. "Do you hate me?"

I stare out at the water and the fishing boats lined up on one side. How can I answer that?

"No, I don't hate you. I wanted to tell you myself at the wake, but I couldn't get you alone. I'm a little bitter that it seems like everyone wants to push me out of town to protect you though."

She nods as though she understands. "I have no idea why I got so angry at the lawyer's office. I'm mad that I was kept in the dark all these years and they were all too chicken to tell me. I took that out on you. If anything, you're the one suffering more than me."

"I think the suffering is the same for both of us, just different." I sigh. "My mom wants me to go home."

"Your mom. That's weird to hear. But of course you have a family. Are they nice? Like, did you enjoy where you grew up?"

I think about it. I might complain about an overprotective mother and a dad who worked more hours than he spent with me, but I wanted for nothing and I never felt unloved. "I did. I love my family, it's just... I expected to get a piece of jewelry or something, not half a building and the opportunity to start a life here."

Clara laughs. "I can understand that. Leave it to Mom to throw a grenade after she dies and stir up the gossip in this town."

"I'd love to know what they were like, but not right now." I'm not sure I could bear hearing about Clara's upbringing right now, imagining how it could've been mine. And most of all, I don't want that to be a part of my decision to stay or not.

"Any time."

"What do you do?" I ask.

"I'm the librarian. One of them at least."

"And you're happy here?"

She nods. "I am."

"Did you go to school for English?" I ask. How ironic that I wanted to major in English but was talked out of it by my dad.

"Yeah. Worthless degree, right?" She chuckles. "But I had a double major, so I took library sciences too."

"I think it's great. I wanted to get an English degree too. I love reading. Of course, I never imagined my own life being similar to a novel."

She chuckles. "Well, Mom thought I should be a doctor or a lawyer. She pushed me to leave Sunrise Bay, and when I returned after college, she was upset with me. She said she never got to see the world and she wanted that for me."

"It's not so great," I say with a shy sort of grin.

"Where are you from?" Clara asks.

"Connecticut. I love the seasons we get there. It's a good place to live. Hell, I have no idea why I'm even entertaining doing something with the building. Maybe I'm bored." I shake my head and cross my arms.

"I can't say enough good things about Sunrise Bay. If you want to stay, I'll abandon my stake and give it to you."

My head whips in her direction. "Clara, no."

She looks at the bay and back at me. "It's the least I can do. I mean, I'm happy you've had a great life and your parents were good to you, but I had my whole life here with your birth parents. You should have a piece of her. That store was a huge part of her life. She worked so much, night and day."

"You must have memories there too?"

She nods. "Yeah, running around while she was teaching ladies how to make their own clothes. Overhearing the gossip. But once I got older, I never really went with her. Like I said, you deserve a piece of her."

"I can't do that. It's both of ours, and I'm probably crazy for thinking I might want to stay. Do Cade and Jed have a point?" I stand and walk closer to the bay, unsure why I'm even asking someone who doesn't know me.

"I think you schooled them pretty good." She chuckles. "I can't tell you what to do, but what does your gut tell you?"

"I'm not sure I should listen to my gut right now."

She tilts her head. "Why?"

"Because it's telling me to prove Cade Greene wrong. Show that I can start this business and be successful and live in this town."

Clara smiles. "Then do it. Nothing has to be written in stone. If it doesn't work out, you can leave, and Sunrise Bay can just be a chapter of your life."

I look at her with a small smile. "Spoken like a true librarian."

She laughs. "I suppose so." Then she sighs. "I'd like to

get to know you better. I know you have your entire family, but I don't have anyone left..." Tears fill her eyes.

I move to touch her but retract, unsure if it's my place.

She's quick to put up her hand and shake her head. "Please do not stay because of me." She wipes her tears. "You don't need to pity me, but even if you leave, would you mind keeping in touch?"

"Not at all. Regardless of our situation, you are my only blood relative."

I used to beg my parents for a sibling. Little did I know I'd get one at the age of twenty-nine. If I stay here, I could get to know Clara. Form a true friendship and maybe a sisterly bond. She's a reason for me to stay, at least temporarily.

As I stand on the edge of a bay in a town far away from my hometown, I take the biggest leap I ever have in my life.

"I think I want to stay," I whisper.

Clara's mitten-covered hand falls into mine and she squeezes. "Then stay."

I guess that's that.

WHEN CLARA and I return from the bay, Cade's coming out of the coffee shop, The Grind.

She touches my forearm to stop us when my eyes lock with his. "He's a good guy, just harbors some... well, you know how when you're younger, things define you—"

I hold up my hand to stop her. "That sounds incredibly too complicated for my life right now." The last thing I need is a man in my life who has more emotional issues than I do.

She shakes her head. "I'm selling him all wrong."

"In my experience, if you have to sell him, there's a problem."

She nods. "True, but he is my best friend's brother, so I feel the need to tell you one small thing about this town."

We walk back into the store, and I'm not gonna lie, I feel a little defeated looking at this mess. "That being?"

"Cade is a Greene and there are a lot of Greenes in Sunrise Bay. So maybe just watch what you say in front of people."

I nod. No talking shit about Cade Greene to anyone. Easy-peasy. I'm not a shit-stirrer anyway.

"I'll help you pack all this up. I might want to keep some stuff if that's okay?" Clara asks.

"Of course." I look up from a pile of patterns. "I really want you to have your money for your half of the building, but I can't afford to buy you out and renovate this place to be what I want it to be. Still, I can't allow you to just give me your half."

She takes a moment and looks around then shrugs. "I don't really care about the building. I mean, it's where my mom did her business, but I have the house, so let's just call it even."

It doesn't sit right with me, so I make a mental note to figure out some way to pay Clara back.

"What are you thinking you want to do with this place anyway?" She sits on a table.

"I think I should do an inventory of what Sunrise Bay already has. And the shops in the neighboring towns."

"Definitely. That's a great idea." She hops off the table. "I can totally—"

We're interrupted when the bell rings. An elderly woman with hair as white as fresh-fallen snow comes in with another woman who has the bluish tint a lot of older women have in their hair, followed by a third woman with dark-rimmed glasses.

"Presley Knight?"

"Grandma Ethel." Clara walks over to the woman with white hair.

My throat closes up. Another grandma I didn't know about?

"Clara dear, how are you? The news just hit Northern Lights Retirement Home, so I told Dori and Midge here, we need to get over there and figure this all out."

Clara laughs. "I'll admit at first—"

She's cut off by Ethel, who approaches me. "You two look so much alike." She holds my upper arms as though she's getting a good look at me. Almost as if she's appraising my worth. It's a tad creepy. "Welcome to Sunrise Bay. I heard Denise left the two of you this building."

"Yeah, Jed and—" Clara gets cut off again.

"Rumor is you might be staying. Opening a place of your own," Ethel says.

I catch the dark-rimmed glasses granny walking around and inspecting the spools of thread, and I watch as she shoves one in her purse. What the heck? "Yeah, I'm not sure what I'm going to do with the space yet."

"Not a sewing store. You're much too young," the one I think is Dori says.

Midge sticks another spool of thread into her purse and my eyes widen.

"Presley was just saying that she was going to go around town and see what we already had, and I suggested that maybe Lake Starlight—"

Grandma Ethel doesn't allow Clara to finish, and Clara huffs at the third interruption.

"That is a great idea. I have just the person to show you around."

"Oh, I was going to Uber or rent a car," I say.

Dori waves. "Duke Thompson doesn't have time to take only one client around all day."

"I could rent..." I stop, seeing Dori's lips twist in displeasure. "Or not?"

"You need someone who knows where to take you," Dori says.

"I can—" Clara raises her hand, but Dori takes Clara's wrist and lowers her arm.

"You're much too busy at the library, Clara dear. I have just the person." Dori looks around the room. "We definitely need to get this project started as soon as possible."

"Um, I think I'd prefer to go by myself," I say.

Grandma Ethel smiles at me. "This is Alaska, dear. You're not familiar with the roads. What happens if something happens to your rental car and you find yourself face-to-face with a bear or, heaven forbid, a moose?"

"Rental cars are never reliable," Dori interjects.

I look at Clara and she shakes her head as though I might as well just give in. I'll admit the bear or moose attack idea is a little scary.

"It's just half a day. Believe me, you'll be happy to have someone show you the ins and outs," Ethel says.

It dawns on me that I have no idea who these two could be offering up to show me around, and hanging out with them might be preferable. "Okay, but maybe you two could show me around? I mean, you must know this area the best."

Ethel looks at Dori and nods. "She has a point."

"She does," Dori says.

"Okay, we heard you're at Glacier Point? We'll be there tomorrow at nine in the morning." Ethel pats my hand.

"Perfect. I'll be ready."

Ethel smiles. "We should go. See you tomorrow, Parsley."

"It's Presley." I smile.

"That's what I said. Maybe wear some sensible shoes too, all right?"

"Okay." I look at my heels.

"But those jeans are keepers." Dori points and places a ten on the table. "For Midge. She's a bit of a kleptomaniac."

They leave the store, and I feel as if I've been run over by a bulldozer.

"What's up with the grandma gang?" I ask Clara.

She's biting her lip, staring after their departure. "That's Ethel Greene and her friend, Dori Bailey. Midge is new. I haven't met her yet."

"Greene as in..."

"Cade Greene's grandma."

"Great."

She laughs. "Well, they do know the area best, but I'd make sure you have your cell phone fully charged. I have no idea where you'll end up."

If Midge comes along, probably the county jail.

Chapter Nine

"See you soon and make sure you
shower and look nice."
~ Ethel Greene

Cade

I'm at the kitchen table, eating breakfast, when Fisher walks in wearing his sheriff's uniform after a long overnight shift.

"You okay, man?"

He nods. "Just beat." He grabs a water. "I'm showering and going to bed."

He disappears upstairs, and I continue scrolling through my phone and eating my eggs. I'm midway through seeing what my high school girlfriend, Reese, posted last night when my phone vibrates, and my grandma's name flashes across the screen.

"Hey, Grandma," I say.

"How's my favorite grandson?" she asks, which means she needs a favor.

"Would no one else answer their phone?"

She laughs. "You're my first choice, always."

"What do you need?" I pick up my plate, rinse it, and put it in the dishwasher.

"Something is wrong with Dori's Cadillac and it won't

start. We promised to take out a friend who's visiting. Could you pick us up and drop us off? We can find a ride home."

"When do you need to be there?" I glance at the time on the microwave because a guy is coming in today to taste a few beers and let us know if he wants them on his shelves. He owns five small grocery stores in the neighboring communities.

"At nine, then you can just drop us off at Two Brothers and an Egg."

"So you want me to come to Lake Starlight and bring you back to Sunrise Bay? Sure." I'll make it back in plenty of time.

"With one pit stop to pick up my friend at Glacier Point."

"Okay."

"Great." She sounds so happy, it makes me go over what she said like I might've missed something, but nothing stands out. "See you soon and make sure you shower and look nice."

"Um, okay?"

"I can't have my friend saying my grandson smells like he works in a brewery." She chuckles at her own joke. "A spritz of cologne would be nice."

"Cologne?" I can't even remember the last time I wore cologne. Jed, on the other hand, has five different bottles, and he plays a game of eeny, meeny, miny, moe with them before he goes anywhere.

"You know how us grandmas are. We like to brag, and I can't brag if you show up looking like a slob."

I'm not sure the last time I embarrassed my grandma, but it's easier to agree with her. "Sure thing."

We say our goodbyes and I hang up.

Jed comes in through the back door after his run, pulling the earbuds out of his ears. "What's up?"

"Nothing. I have to go pick up Grandma and take her and her friends to breakfast."

His eyebrows rise. "Have fun with that. I'm showering and heading to the brewery. I think I'm going to book some appointments up north to pitch the new beer. Do you think you can handle the town council meeting on your own?"

"Yeah, sure."

"Okay, it's at the end of the week and I know they're going to be talking about Mrs. Harrison's business. If blondie wants to open something, she'll have to tell them and get their approval. This might just be the nail in her coffin."

I shake my head at Jed because he's got a one-track mind. "We don't even know what she plans to do with it."

"I saw her and Clara yesterday and they looked tight, so I'm pretty sure Presley's sweet-talked her into cooperating." He gulps down a green smoothie he had in the fridge. "Xavier said Clara told him that she gave her half of the building to Presley."

"I'm heading out. We can discuss this later."

Jed just needs to give up the fight at this point.

"You're only being this way because you want her," he says.

I shake my head. "I did, but I ruined my chance."

I'm not going to divulge to Jed that I'm beating off to imaginings of Presley at night. That she was the first woman in a long time who interested me. Because all he can see is that building and how he can't have what he wants. Presley is in the way of that, so she's the devil.

"She's not worth it anyway. I mean, yeah, her ass is out

of this fucking world, but..." Jed stops and narrows his eyes. "Fuck no."

"What?"

"You still want her. I just saw that jealous look flash in your eyes when I talked about her ass."

Adam walks in, looking like he woke from a long hibernation about a minute ago.

"I have no idea what you're talking about."

Jed hits Adam in the arm, and Adam actually moves his hand over his bicep like it hurt. The guy is a forest ranger and in a helluva lot better shape than either of us. "Look at Cade."

Adam stops in front of the fridge. "What am I looking at?" His voice is still groggy.

"You know that new chick in town, Presley? Man, I want to bend her over, put both my hands on that ass of hers, and get to grinding."

Adam laughs, the first one I've heard from him in weeks.

Jed's smug grin says I've proved him right. "See? Told you. She's our enemy, man."

I raise my hands in the air.

Adam opens the fridge and pulls out a batch of wings I brought home last night after we closed. He bites into one and goes back upstairs.

Jed and I both follow Adam's movements until he disappears.

"I'm gonna call for an intervention if he's not in the angry phase by next week," he says.

"She left him with no explanation other than she wasn't happy. Give him a break." I grab my jacket from the hook by the back door. "I'm out of here."

"Don't get lost and end up licking Presley's honey pot, okay?"

I shake my head and shut the door before he can say anything else that will give me visuals to add to my spank bank.

I PICK up Grandma Ethel and Dori from the Northern Lights Retirement Center. They each have their own apartments there, and since Dori can't drive anymore, Grandma drives Dori's Cadillac. Dori is actually Doris Bailey, owner of Bailey Timber Corp, the largest timber company in the state. She comes from as big of a family as we do, except they're not a blended family like mine.

"So nice of you to pick us up, Cade," Dori says, climbing into the back of my truck.

Grandma hops in right after, next to Dori, leaving me as their chauffeur with no one in the front passenger seat.

"Um. Grandma?" I ask.

"Oh, our friend will sit there so she can see the sights. I'm old and I can't be moving around so much. The more I get up and down from your truck, the more likely I'll break a hip. And then someone will have to wipe my ass. Do you want that job, Cade?"

I wince and decide that instead of arguing, I'll just get on my way. I put the truck in drive to get this favor over with.

On the way to Glacier Point, I endure a conversation about nutritional shakes and which ones help them stay regular. I might have zoned out. I pull up in the circular entrance and do a double take when I see Presley standing outside. She's got on another great pair of jeans, but instead of the high heels, she's in a pair of boots. A jacket covers up whether she's got on another tight sweater.

"Do I need to go in and get your friend?" I ask, hardly taking my eyes off Presley. She's checking her phone and hasn't looked up yet.

"No, she's right there." Dori rolls down her window. "Yoo-hoo."

Presley picks up her head and smiles at Dori before she takes in the truck and sees me through the windshield. Then the smile is quickly stripped from her face. She walks toward the truck, but doesn't get in.

"I'm sorry, I think there was a misunderstanding. I thought it would only be us three." Presley never even looks at me.

"Sorry, my car didn't start, so we called Ethel's grandson. Presley, this is Cade."

"We've met," she says through a tight smile. "Let's just reschedule."

"Nonsense, go sit up front." Dori waves at the valet. "Excuse me, I'm Wyatt's grandma-in-law. Can you please open the door for this woman?"

The guy actually comes over and opens the door, but Presley doesn't step in. Her jaw twists, and little huffs fall from her mouth. It's a turn-on, watching her be so defiant. Makes me want to throw her over my shoulder and drag her home.

"Ma'am," the valet says.

"Yeah, yeah, I'm coming." She climbs up, still not looking at me. "I don't have a ton of time anyway."

"Good, me either. I'm just dropping you at breakfast. Surely you can handle a twenty-minute car ride with me?"

She looks at my grandma in the back. "I thought we were looking around the different towns?"

I look in the rearview mirror and find Grandma hitting Dori on the arm.

"Oh, I have to go. That's Wyatt and my great-grandson." Dori points out the window, but I don't see who she could be talking about. "I completely forgot I said I'd watch him this morning." She opens the door, and since the valet is still nearby, he helps her down. "Cade, you don't mind if I steal your grandma, do you? I could really use her help. I can't watch a toddler all by myself. He'll have me tied to a chair or will be running out in the middle of traffic. You don't want a child running into the middle of traffic on your conscience, do you?"

"Sorry, dear." Grandma pats my shoulder. "But you two go. Cade knows all the places around here too."

"I'll definitely just do this another time." Presley's hand goes to the door handle.

"Nonsense." Dori is suddenly at Presley's door as though she's strong enough to keep it shut if Presley tries anything.

I'm not a complete idiot. I know the stories of Dori involving herself in her grandchildren's love lives. And now it looks as though they think they're going to involve themselves in mine. That's a no-go.

"Let her go if she wants." I spread my arm out along the seat of my truck, my other hand on the steering wheel. "It's just that she can't control herself around me." I laugh.

Presley doesn't. "That's not it. Surely you have better things to do rather than take me around town."

Both grandmas peer through the window, waiting to make sure we pull out of here.

"Actually, I have about an hour," I say. "Can you handle an hour in my presence without jumping my bones?"

She guffaws, and I want to clap myself on the back for earning that reaction. "Of course I can."

"Good, then you two go." Grandma waves. "Bye now."

They both go inside the resort, probably to have a long leisurely brunch.

"You can just take me to the store, and I'll figure it out after that." She's facing forward, her purse in her lap with her hands holding it to her body.

"I can drive you around. It's not a problem."

She turns toward me. "Did you plan this? Have your grandma set this up?"

"Why would I do that?"

"So you can be a little birdy in my ear about how I'm not going to be successful and I should just let you and your brother bail me out."

I laugh. "Man, that's a conniving thought. One thing you'll figure out fast if you move here is that my grandma noses her way into everyone's business. Dori's her sidekick. Those two have already gotten her grandchildren married off. They must think we make a good couple."

She scoffs. "They don't even know me."

"I'm not saying they're right. I'm just stating a fact."

She turns and narrows her eyes. "Can we please just go?"

"Nothing would make me happier." I pull out of Glacier Point and turn right toward Lake Starlight's downtown.

"Where are you going? Isn't Sunrise Bay that way?" She points in the opposite direction.

"I'm showing you around here first."

"Why?"

"Because I'm a nice guy, even if you don't believe me."

She huffs, but her attitude dies down a bit. "Well, thank you. I'll gladly pay you for gas."

I shake my head. "That's okay, I'll just take it off what we pay you for the building."

Her head whips my way and a strand of her blonde hair sticks to her lip gloss. She's quick to pull it away.

"I'm kidding," I say.

The tension leaves her body, but damn, she's strung so tight right now. When we reach a stoplight, I pick up my phone and text Jed that I won't be at the meeting this afternoon, but I fail to mention the reason why.

Chapter Ten

"See? I can fix your problems."
~ Cade Greene

Presley

Cade drives slowly down Main Street in Lake Starlight. I try to concentrate on the diner, the tattoo shop, the bakery. Anything but the way his long fingers flex on the steering wheel. The way he taps out a song with only four fingers on his muscular thighs that flex under his jeans. The fact that there's a scent in his truck. It's not a specific cologne or left-overs rotting in the back. It's a fresh scent that I'm scared might be Cade's signature smell. Scared because I like it a little too much and I hope it permeates my own clothes.

"So is this like recon work?" he asks, passing the restaurant he was going to take me to the other night. The maroon awnings with Terra and Mare in gold makes it look like a fancy restaurant. I wonder how different things would be between us right now had he not canceled.

"I just want to make sure I don't venture into something that has stiff competition."

"Makes sense." He continues inching along the street. It must be driving the people behind us crazy. After Lake

Starlight, he follows a sign to Greywall. "There are three towns pretty close together around here. So if whatever you want to do isn't in one of those, maybe you've found your niche. I think it's smart to do inventory of what's around, but what do *you* want to do?"

Do I really want to sit in a car and have Cade try to figure me out? It sounds dangerous.

"I honestly don't know."

"What do you enjoy doing?" he asks.

I think back to my life in Connecticut. After college, I had a slew of jobs in offices that I loathed. I didn't enjoy sitting at a desk for an entire day—or worse, being in meetings where I swear people droned on because they enjoyed hearing their own voices more than they had something useful to say. I can't count how many times I sat in those meetings thinking *this should have been an email.*

"Okay, let's start with the basics," he says. "What do you do in your free time?"

"Um..."

"Any hobbies?"

I shake my head.

"All right, I guess I'll make it even easier. If you have a night free, do you go out or stay in?"

"Stay in probably," I say.

"Do you cook or get takeout?"

"Get takeout."

"So you can't cook?" Cade glances over.

"Kind of. Simple stuff, but I wouldn't enjoy spending my entire night cooking and washing dishes."

"So a cooking school is out of the question." He smiles as if he's saying, "See? I can fix your problems."

I raise both eyebrows.

He grins. "Television show or movie?"

"Neither," I say. "I'd read."

"There you go. On the couch or in the bathtub?" he asks.

"How is that going to help you figure out what would make me happy?"

"It's not. I was just hoping you said bathtub so I could get a visual."

I playfully push his arm and he exaggerates the hit, going up against the glass of his window. I roll my eyes. "Nice."

"Sounds like maybe books is a possibility. There's one bookstore in Greywall. I'll drive you by it. We can go in if you want."

Books? I let that thought resonate for a moment. I do enjoy reading. Always have. And I did want to take English in college before I let myself be railroaded into getting a business degree. A bookstore might be nice. But so many people read off of e-readers nowadays. Would I stand a chance of being successful?

"There are libraries for books," I say out loud when I didn't mean to.

"True, but bookstores are popular even with libraries around. Have been for decades."

He pulls into downtown Greywall and I immediately see where the town got its name. Whereas the mountains in Sunrise Bay are in the distance and at the far side of the water, here the town is set at the base of them and it serves to act as a giant gray wall rising up behind the town. It makes me feel little. I lean forward to look in wonder out of the windshield so I can see the top.

He parks along the curb just outside the bookstore, which just says "Books" on the window. Cade turns off the ignition and climbs out of his truck. I quickly follow him, and he's a gentleman, opening the store door for me. Walking in, I'm very aware that he's behind me and could be checking out my ass. A blush warms my cheeks as I politely say hello to the man behind the counter.

As I head down an aisle of shelves, Cade detours straight to the man and says, "Can I ask you a question?"

"Sure."

Cade leans on the counter as though they're friends. "Has the whole e-book business hurt you?"

The man stands from his chair. If he has a chair, does that mean he's not nearly as busy as he should be? "I sell a lot of travel books on the area. Lots of nonfiction. Greywall's library isn't great, so for our residents who don't want to venture down to Anchorage, this store is a good one to come to. All in all, I would say no."

"Great. Thanks." Cade shakes the guy's hand and joins me in the second aisle.

The guy wasn't joking about nonfiction. His fiction shelves are sparse and his children's section nonexistent. For a moment, the Shop Around the Corner from the movie *You've Got Mail* comes to mind. What a great way to fill your day. Story time and helping kids learn to love to read.

"You know, I think I met you about ten years ago," Cade says from behind me.

I stop and circle around. "Excuse me?"

I haven't forgotten the one other time I was in Sunrise Bay. My parents never knew I came until my dad received my credit card bill. I was nineteen and Grandma Beatrice had just passed away. My mom said it wasn't my place to come pay my respects, that the family didn't know me. And that's when I showed up and found out about Clara.

He nods. "At the cemetery. I think you were visiting your grandmother's grave."

"That was you?" It all comes back to me. He was younger, more boy than man, and he mistakenly thought I was Clara.

He nods. "It was me. So you knew about everything for a long time?"

Just thinking about that moment in my life makes me wish I would've listened to my mom. No one knew I was here, and when I saw my biological parents hugging Clara, the pain was immense.

"Yeah. Ready?" I walk out of the aisle, past the man. "Thank you so much. Great store."

He says bye and I walk out onto the sidewalk, staring at a cupcake shop. I'm not gonna lie, I wouldn't mind buying a dozen, sitting down on the park bench, and stuffing my face until the pain just goes away.

Cade comes out and unlocks the truck. He tries to open the door for me, but as soon as he hits the key fob, I grab the handle.

Before I shut the door, I turn to face him. "Can you just take me back to Sunrise Bay?"

He nods and rounds the back of the truck. Just as I was starting to warm up to him, he had to go and bring up something painful.

CADE DROPS me off at the sewing store without saying much else. During the drive to Sunrise Bay, I came to the conclusion that a bookstore would be a great way to earn a living. But I'd need to cash in my 401k from my job in order to afford to renovate. My dad would never give me a loan. Even if he entertained it, Mom would say hell no, hoping it would drive me back to Connecticut.

So after I get some large garbage bags from Handyman Haven and get rid of some of the stuff I'm positive Clara won't want, I stop the anxiety brewing inside me, deciding it's time to call home and tell my parents my plan. The last thing I want is my mom showing up in Sunrise Bay. I dial and put the phone on speaker.

My mom answers immediately, as she usually does. "Presley, how are things?"

"Good."

"When are you coming home? I was just talking to—"

"Mom."

She's silent. She knows. The woman knows me better than I know myself. She never could get pregnant, but her motherly instincts never fail her. "You're staying."

See? I told you. I inhale a deep breath, waiting for the inevitable lecture. "I have to."

"You don't have to," she says coldly.

I know she's hurt, and she's scared. But I hope she can see this as something I need to do. "I want to. I want to start over and find my place in the world, carve out a life for myself."

"Then go to Boston, go to New York. Start over closer to home. You don't have to start over in their town."

My heart breaks for my mom. "This is where the opportunity is. Clara gave me her half, although I'd really like to pay her back. I'm going to cash in my 401k so that I can renovate the space. I want to open a bookstore and gear it toward fiction. Have a kids section and a teen section. Get kids wanting to read early."

I plead my best case. Mom was the driving force behind me becoming a reader. She pushed me when my literacy was lower than average. She's the one who spurred the love of the written word inside me.

"You always loved your books. Are you sure that's not what you're doing now, sweetie?"

"What do you mean?" I ask, rolling a spool of thread back and forth under my fingers on the table.

"I think you enjoy living in those books, imagining yourself in those situations. You'd gush for hours about them. Are you sure you staying there and starting over isn't you trying to write a new book for yourself?"

Even though the silence is deafening, I think over what she's saying. "I'm not a Knight here. I'm just Presley, the love child Denise Harrison gave up for adoption."

"Exactly! That's like a scarlet letter in a small town, Pres."

"I can handle it. I've handled worse."

She's quiet, but I hear her spoon stirring in her teacup. I glance at my phone to see the time, and yeah, this is her tea time every day. Memories of when she would pour a cup and pick up a book while I read beside her on the couch come rushing back.

"It's okay, Mom. I'm going to be okay here." I truly do believe that. The conversation with Clara went pretty well. I could do without Ethel manipulating me to spend a day with her grandson. Although he's the one who brought up the idea of me having a bookstore.

I wish I could shake whatever this is I feel for him.

"At least let me come up and help you get set up," she says.

"I can't let you do that. I want to do it on my own."

If my mom comes, she'll bulldoze me, and this store will end up being what she wants. The need to strike out on my own is like a match that's been lit inside me. That little flame is growing into a raging fire I can't put out.

"At least let me come to the grand opening?"

I smile. "Of course."

"And we'll be sending you over half the money for Clara. You can pay us back."

"Mom, no." I never expected her to be this okay with my move.

"I know you, and you'll give in to suggestions she gives you or do something to make her happy. If this is really going to be yours, it's going to be yours. So just pay her and you can pay us back."

"With interest?" I ask.

"Sure," she says.

I know they might not pressure me to pay them back, but I'm going to pay every dime—eventually.

"Mom," I say. She doesn't say anything. I'm sure she's still processing. "Thank you so much."

"You're my daughter. Your happiness is my happiness."

I smile, knowing how fortunate I am to have her. Then guilt weighs on me because why do I feel the need to get to know the woman who gave me up?

"Now do what Knights do. Take that city by storm and show them they don't scare you."

I laugh. "I will."

We hang up, and I lean back in the chair. Too far back apparently, because it tilts all the way and I fall to the floor. Even though I'm staring at the ceiling, I finally feel as though all the pieces are coming together.

A paper gets shoved into the slot of the door, so I stand, walk over, and pick it up. Another dose of dread replaces my excitement.

Town meeting Thursday night.
On the agenda:
Parking meters by the bay.

Fourth of July fireworks.
Denise Harrison's building.
Seven p.m.

Great. I can only assume the Greene brothers are responsible for this one. I'll be sure to thank them.

Chapter Eleven

"Let's not play games."
- Presley Knight

Cade

Thursday night comes faster than I hoped. Mostly because there's nothing I can do at the town meeting to stop Presley's plans. Jed's on my ass about voting no, but she's got Clara in her back pocket so everyone will agree that a bookstore, which I heard she ultimately did decide to go with, is a great addition to the Sunrise Bay downtown area.

I walk into the town building on the other side of the square and the room is already packed, thanks to Nikki announcing to everyone what's happening tonight. Usually it's only the business owners within the square who care what kind of business comes in. Mostly they're worried someone is going to sell sex toys or that wacky weed as George refers to it.

Most of the council members are sitting along the panel already, but there's no sign of Presley, so I linger outside. I can't even answer why. The woman hates me. She's started cleaning out the shop and I tried to help her with a table she was struggling to get out the door. Her response was to tell me to stay on my side of the sidewalk.

Just as I second-guess my decision and am about to go in and find my seat, I spot Presley walking up the sidewalk with Clara next to her. Man, they sure have become chummy.

"Cade." Clara walks by me.

"Clara."

She smirks because I'm sure Clara is very aware of my feelings for Presley. It isn't every day I show interest in a woman.

"Mr. Greene." Presley never looks at me.

I clasp her elbow lightly to stop her from going inside. "Mr. Greene is my father."

"Sorry to offend you. I really need to get in there." She finally looks at me.

"There's something I want you to know before you go in there."

An expression of boredom lands on her face and she sighs. I'm half tempted to say fuck it and keep what I was going to say to myself rather than be honest.

Instead, I say, "The board only cares about tourism season. Make sure you use that to make your case and you're in."

"Oh gee, thanks. I'm so happy I ran into you, otherwise I would've bombed this presentation."

Her sarcasm does nothing but make my dick harden. And just for that, I'm not going to tell her that I get a vote.

"Then by all means, knock their socks off." I hold my arm out and she walks away without so much as a thanks.

Presley heads inside, and with us blessed with an unusually mild spring night, I realize I'm going to be tortured by a view of her legs for the next several months.

Her ass in jeans was spectacular, but her legs in a skirt... damn. I might as well fall on my knees and beg her to forgive me now.

After she leaves, my dad walks up the steps and clasps me on the shoulder. "Cade."

"Hey, Dad."

"It's funny. I heard something about you and a certain soon-to-be bookstore owner." He laughs. "Nikki sure can spread the gossip."

"Maybe she should use her voice on the radio for something more productive than igniting rumors."

He laughs. After he married Marla, my dad truly did take on her kids as his own. Although they have a father, he rarely comes up to Sunrise Bay. After the affair, all their relationships with him became strained. "They aren't rumors if it's the truth. I like the idea of you falling for someone."

"I haven't fallen. She just piques my interest."

We take the hallway along the side of the large room to the door on the side.

"Still, after seeing you dodge relationships for the past decade or so, it's a nice change."

"Don't go counting grandkids," I say. "This isn't anything serious. We haven't even been on a date."

He stops before we head through the door. "Son, I know that with losing your mom, it's hard to be vulnerable and let someone in, but one day you're going to have to."

My dad is the kind of man you can talk to about anything. Before my mom died, he was always there for us in regard to playing and joking around. But after Mom died, he really became our confidante. I guess he didn't have much of a choice though.

"Who says?"

He blows out a breath and puts his hand on my shoulder as though he's ready to give me a long talk. Instead, the gavel on the desk announces the meeting is about to start. Instead of talking to me, Dad reaches for the door and opens it.

He rounds the back of the panel, finding his seat next to George Lehman, the head of the Downtown Business District Committee. My dad doesn't have a storefront but he's on the committee because he's a longtime resident with a respectable business and often acts as a tie-breaker on votes. He's our impartial third party, you could say.

I find my seat next to Trent Lawson, and as I lower to sit in my chair, my gaze falls to Presley in the first row. Her mouth slowly drops open, and I bite my inner cheek before my smile forms. Having to stare at those crossed legs the entire meeting... all I can do is be grateful the desk hides my lower half from view.

I'm not sure who will be more tortured during this town council meeting: her or me.

***

GEORGE IS A LIST MAKER, so when the flyers went out, everyone knew the meeting would start with parking meters and whether we should extend the time. Then we moved into the Fourth of July fireworks—how much will be spent, whether we have to change them, the regulations on boats in the bay during the show. There are no objections from anyone. Fourth of July is a huge day for us in Sunrise Bay.

Coming to the discussion of Denise Harrison's building, George calls up Presley. She has Clara help her set up her computer and dim the lights.

My dad leans over George to whisper to me, "A slide show? I like this girl."

"Don't call the church just yet, Dad."

Trent laughs. "She's a spitfire. She'd keep you on your toes." He nudges me with his elbow.

I refrain from telling them they're all crazy.

"Okay, so these are just some ideas I had," Presley says, "and how I see the building looking inside and out. And I'm going to be really focused on running events and promotions that would drive traffic into Sunrise Bay, especially during tourist season." She eyes me when she says that, and Trent and my dad glance over.

She flips on the video, and as soon as it begins I wonder how much time and money she put into this. A simple sketch would have gotten her in. The video scans past Truth or Dare Brewery to what she envisions her building looking like. It's got the navy blue awning but printed with The Story Shop. The camera continues through the double doors and she's added little streams of stars as though it's magic that we're stepping into. The store is quaint and cute and everything Sunrise Bay residents and tourists eat up. Circular tables full of displays, floor-to-ceiling bookshelves closer to the front and filled with books. But midway through the building, it turns into a children's paradise. Small toadstools spread around an apple tree painted on the wall, lower bookshelves for the kids to grab their own books that interest them. There's a section for young adult fiction to the right with monthly book recommendations and a couch and chair.

I haven't put too much thought into the upbringing Presley had. Based on her fancy clothes, I assume she came from money. But she clearly went to school for *something* because her sales pitch is pretty damn good.

After the video ends, she goes through all the bullet points on why she thinks her bookstore will be a great addition to the downtown area. It all holds up and I can't see why anyone would say no. In truth, the fact that any new business that wants to come into the square needs to be approved by a vote from the five chairs on the committee is ridiculous. But that's small-town life.

Since Jed and I share a chair on the committee and I'm the one here tonight, I vote how I see fit. We all write down our votes and hand them to George. Presley's foot bounces up and down as she waits for the answer. Clara smiles at her and nods confidently.

"Okay, the votes are in. It's four to one in approval of Denise Harrison's sewing store becoming The Story Shop. Congratulations." George sets the votes down in front of him. "May I suggest that you read all the by-laws that will impact the awning you want to install and read up on the rules for window displays and sidewalk promotions in the square?"

Presley smiles. "Thank you so much." She nods to everyone, purposely skipping me it seems. "I promise The Story Shop will be a success."

"I'm sure it will, Miss Knight." George nods, and half of me wonders if they all approved it just so gossip will continue to swirl around Presley and me. "Now, does anyone have any other line of business we need to discuss?"

Zoe from The Grind raises her hand and gets the go-ahead to ask her question. "I'm wondering about the duo night. When will we hear which two businesses will be partnering up next?"

George looks at my dad, and they both glance at me. I'm fairly sure the brewery will be one of the two since we haven't been chosen in a while, and we'll probably be paired with Trent Lawson. We've already discussed him giving free legal advice and we'd name a beer after him for the month.

After having a silent conversation with my dad, George says, "Let's tackle that in two weeks."

Zoe raises her hand again.

"Yes, Zoe," George says.

Zoe was my mom's business partner when they opened The Grind. I'm not sure how much of the business my dad still owns or whether he's allowed Zoe to buy him out. He never involves himself in it anymore. I love Zoe, but every time I see her, I think of Mom and her hopes and dreams when they started the small coffee shop.

Zoe stands. "I mention it because I was thinking that The Grind and The Story Shop would be a great pairing."

George looks at my father again. There might be three other people on this committee but my dad and George run things.

"We'll take that into account." George looks around. "Anything else?"

My gaze falls to my sisters Mandi and Posey in the front row. One runs a B&B and the other runs Fringe, the haircutting salon. I always joke that the brewery should team up with Fringe for a night. But no one gets a choice. The committee decides and lately, they've enjoyed more absurd than perfect pairings. Hence Bakey Cakey and Chuck's Meatmarket being paired up for the last one.

"Meeting adjourned." George slams down the gavel, which I'm pretty sure isn't really needed but he uses it only because he loves doing it.

I head down from the panel and get hung up with Mandi asking me whether the brewery has any more of the peach flavored beer available for her. It was a best seller last year at her B&B.

After they pack up, Clara comes over and brings Presley with her. "Presley, this is Mandi and Posey Greene."

They all shake hands, briefly discussing their businesses.

"Sorry about Nikki," Posey says.

So far it's been like a Presley Knight biography this week on Nikki's show.

"It's better not to listen," I say.

"I'm fine." Presley sets her gaze on me. She almost has this look like she's daring me to try to break her. "It's nothing I haven't dealt with before."

"Congratulations," I say, trying to turn the conversation to happier matters.

"Thanks." She straightens her computer bag on her shoulder. I'd usually volunteer to take it from her, but I get the sense she doesn't want me to help her with anything. "I'm assuming it's no thanks to you. Four to one." She raises an eyebrow.

Mandi purses her lips to stop from smiling, and Posey watches with rapt attention. My two stepsisters, who would love nothing more than to see me get schooled by a woman.

"Why do you assume it was me who voted no?" I ask.

She tilts her head. "Let's not play games." She turns to Mandi and Posey. "It was really nice meeting you. Maybe we could talk about including some promotional materials in each other's businesses."

"Definitely. I keep a small library of books in my B&B, so let's talk," Mandi says.

They all say their goodbyes, and Presley turns to me last. "Bye, Cade," she says as though she doesn't want to be polite, but good manners have been instilled in her and are just a part of who she is.

"Great presentation. Sweet dreams, Presley."

She gives me a seething glare and turns around, quickly heading out of the building—almost as if she's running away from something.

Chapter Twelve

"Just think of how accessible you are with
the flick of a clasp."
~ Cade Greene

Presley

I've sold the final sewing machine, and once it's out of the store, I finally feel as though things are coming together. After discussing with a few people around town who I should hire for the renovation work, it's unanimous that Hank Greene is the man. He's got a team which I'm hoping does not include a Greene family member spending time with me all day while I get the place looking like a bookstore.

A knock sounds on the back door. Since I'm expecting Hank Greene, I open the door without looking, wearing my overalls and sneakers, a bandana around my head. Not my finest look by any means. But it's not Hank Greene, rather his eldest son, Cade.

"Sorry, my dad tried to call you," he says with a grin.

I dig into the front pocket of my overalls for my phone. Shit, I had it on silent. There's a notification that I have a voicemail.

"Thanks." I move to shut the door, but he puts his foot in, stopping me. I open the door back up. "What?"

"My dad asked if I could measure a few things. It's in the message." He walks in with a tape measure in his hand. "It won't take me long."

There's that scent again. The scent of *him*. The one that makes me want to release all the anger I have toward him while he fucks me against the wall. Oh God, what is wrong with me? The man is probably hoping I'll fail so he can get this building for a steal.

"Do you work for your dad?" I ask.

"I'm not on the payroll if that's what you mean." He doesn't even look at me while he measures the front window and jots down notes on a pad of paper. "He just needs to know the specifics so he can order what you need. He's held up at the courthouse, getting the blueprints for the building. Which you'd know if you listened to your messages."

I roll my eyes. "I forgot my phone was on silent."

"Good thing for you I'm right next door," he says, those perfectly white teeth shining bright.

He continues to measure, not paying me any attention. For whatever reason, that annoys me. It shouldn't. I've been doing my best not to pay him an ounce of attention since the day of the committee meeting.

"I'm sure you have your own work to do at the brewery."

He shrugs. "Jed's there. And it's our slow time of the year. We work more on packaging and distribution during the off-season. That, and developing new flavors. Can you give me a hand for a second?" He holds out the end of the measuring tape. "Hold it there." He moves all the way to the other side of the room. "Thanks, you can let go." I do, and he smirks like I tried to get it to snap back at him. "Are you replacing the windows?"

"I think so."

"Just so you know, there are ordinances about which kind you get. But I'm sure you have all that paperwork."

I glance at my file folder on the one lonely table I kept. "Yes."

"I was meaning to ask you the other night before you rushed out, did you go to school for that?"

I grab the edge of the measuring tape, figuring if I help him, he's more likely to get out of here faster. "What's that?"

"The video. It was really good."

"And yet it still didn't entice you to vote yes."

He stops measuring and I release the tape because just the reminder that he voted against me makes me upset.

He sets down the measuring tape and the pad of paper on the floor as he walks toward me, his eyes never wavering from mine. "You need to stop assuming things."

"So you weren't the no vote?"

"Votes are kept confidential. I can't in good faith tell you how I voted because then you'll throw your animosity at one of the other four people. And since I'm the aim of your anger right now, we'll just keep it that way because I'm more forgiving than most."

"Forgiving?"

"Yeah, once you realize I'm a good guy." His Adam's apple bobs as he swallows, his vision dipping to the front of my overalls. "I like the outfit."

"Don't make fun."

He chuckles and his fingers go to one of the clasps. "I'm not making fun. Just think of how accessible you are with the flick of a clasp. You should think about that when you wear them."

I swallow audibly and he chuckles, getting the reaction he hoped for. I'm visualizing what would happen if he did that to me right now and how the material would puddle at my ankles, leaving me in a tight white T-shirt and my panties.

"Well, they're comfortable." I shrug, trying to play off my reaction.

His thumb runs over the metal as if it's taking every ounce of his control not to unclasp it. "That's a great reason."

He lets go and the flood of disappointment is damaging to my psyche. *You can't have him, Presley. Remember Clara's word, complicated. Your life is already a clusterfuck.*

"That's all the measurements I need. My dad should be here soon." He steps away and picks up his measuring tape and pad of paper.

With his back to me, I answer his question because apparently part of me wants to prolong his departure. "I went to school for business. A friend helped me with the video. I did part of it myself and I sketched what I was thinking, but she put it all together."

Emery did an amazing job and I can't take credit for it, even if she'd never know.

"Still, all the statistics and stuff, that was you?" He stops at the door.

I nod.

"Well, great job. Even if it may or may not have swayed me to vote yes." He chuckles and opens the door.

"Cade!" A man strikingly similar to Cade stands on the other side.

"Hey, Dad. Adam?"

Two men walk into the shop and Cade doesn't leave.

"I'm glad Cade got ahold of you. I'm sorry, I hate being

late." Hank Greene puts out his hand and I shake it, envisioning what Cade will look like when he's older. Pretty damn close to this man, I suspect. "This is Adam, Cade's brother."

The younger version of Cade shakes my hand.

"What are you doing here?" Cade asks.

"Adam's gonna help me with this project because he needs to keep busy." Hank turns from Cade to me. "He's a forest ranger, so he'll be here on his off days. I'll fill in on the other days."

"Seriously? You agreed to this?" Cade asks Adam.

Adam shrugs. He shoots a look at Cade, and Cade backs off. I've figured out in the short time I've been here that their family has entire conversations without words, whether it's a flick of an eyebrow or quirk of a lip.

"Cade, do you have the measurements?" Hank takes the piece of paper Cade tears off his pad. "Perfect."

Hank walks around the space and I follow as he asks me questions about what I was thinking for the space. When we're by the windows, discussing the special ones I'll need, my gaze ventures to the back where Cade and Adam now stand, having a conversation. It looks serious.

"Don't mind my sons," Hank whispers. "Adam"—he looks back, and I assume it's to make sure he's not listening —"is going through heartbreak. But he's qualified, don't you worry. He's been my little helper his entire life. He can drywall the holes and repaint. When it comes to the built-in bookshelves, I'll be here to make sure everything is done properly. Adam can probably handle the flooring as well."

He lost me after heartbreak.

"He's young to be so brokenhearted," I say. Damn it, that was supposed to stay inside my head and not come out of my mouth.

Hank nods. "Yeah, well, when you marry your high school sweetheart, the odds are stacked against you. Though I married mine."

I assume he was on the wrong end of those statistics too, because I know he and Marla have a blended family.

"Unfortunately, she passed." He glances at his boys again. "Cade was only twelve. Adam six. I blame myself for letting Adam marry Lucy. They were too young. I think he wanted to repeat what his mother and I had. He's always idealized our relationship. Not that he doesn't love Marla, but it's complicated." He glances at them again. "Neither of my boys would be happy that I'm sharing all this with you, but you'll find out eventually anyway. Maybe I feel bad because my stepdaughter is spreading all the news about your life on her radio show. Tit for tat and all that." He smiles, and jeez, Cade is such a mini-me, even down to the smile.

"It's okay. It's no different in Connecticut. It's nice to actually know what they're saying about me instead of it all being behind my back."

"Well." Hank sits on the windowsill. "I'm pretty sure I speak for the town when I say we're glad you're here and that this bookstore will be a great addition."

So he voted yes then. It has to be Cade. A handyman wouldn't care about my bookstore—hell, I'm giving him business. Trent Lawson will make money on legal fees with me setting up my business. And the fifth person is that woman who I think owns the knickknack store. Maybe she didn't want me here, but she stopped me the other day and asked if I'd have romance novels. It could have been George I suppose but I'd put money on it being Cade who voted no.

"Well, thank you, Mr. Greene."

He stands. "Any time. You look like you're ready to start now. Let me get a quote going..."

"Oh, I can cut you a check."

He waves me off. "Just hold off on that. I'll grab you the quote first."

"I'm really anxious to get this going." I'm not going to divulge that I need to get this store open so I can actually make some money.

He chuckles. "Okay, well, we can start the drywall repair and paint tomorrow." He presses some numbers on his calculator and gives me a figure that I write him a check for. "I gave you a discount on account of you having to deal with my mother trying to push you and Cade together. She's a meddler and her friend Dori isn't any different."

I laugh. "It's okay. I actually have a whole box of spools of thread and fabric. I'm not sure if they'd want it, but Midge helped herself to three spools the other day."

His shoulders deflate and he shakes his head. "I'm not surprised."

I wave off his concern. "Dori paid for it, not that I wanted any money."

"I think they'd love it." He turns away from me. "Cade."

Cade walks over and Adam follows. "Yeah?"

"Presley has a box of thread and fabric that needs to go to Northern Lights. You know your grandma is in that sewing club. They could use it."

"Oh no." I shake my head. "I can do it. I'm staying in Lake Starlight. I can just stop there on my way home."

Hank tucks his clipboard under his arm and holds up his hands. "Now, I'm not meaning you're not strong enough when I say this, because if I were, Marla would be over here and smacking me on the back of the head in an instant. But let Cade do it. Where are you staying in Lake Starlight?"

"Um. Glacier Point."

"Fancy," Adam says under his breath.

My cheeks redden in embarrassment. "I'm looking to stay someplace else. I didn't know where to stay when I first came. It's just a lot of things in Sunrise Bay are houses for rent and they're all looking for long-term leases. I'm not ready for that kind of commitment just yet."

"I have a place," Hank says and turns to his sons as if he's getting their opinion. Adam raises his eyebrows as though his dad is crazy and Cade's eyes slowly shut. "The boys live in my old house. Above the garage, there's a small apartment. We used it for guests back in the day. You're welcome to stay there."

"Oh no. I don't think that's a good idea." I shake my head, eyes wide.

"Why not? You're a client and I treat my clients like family. I haven't been up there in a while, so I'll have the boys clear it out. But I can't imagine how hard it is for you to upheave your entire life to come here. You'll have to get a car and this place is costing a small fortune. Think of it as a welcome wagon gift."

Cade chokes but recovers before his dad notices. The whole welcome wagon discussion from before rings in my head.

"I'll think about it," I say.

"Okay, I don't want to force it on you," Hank says. "But just a disclaimer, it's out of the boys' area. It has its own bathroom and kitchen, so you'd never have to see their mugs unless you wanted to do laundry in the main. I'll install black-out curtains myself, so they don't act like peeping toms."

"Dad!" Cade screeches.

I giggle at how he turned into a thirteen-year-old boy at his dad's remark.

"I better get to my next appointment. I can't go getting bad Yelp reviews." Hank laughs all the way out the door, stopping short when he sees the boxes. "Cade, don't forget these boxes."

"I won't."

Adam and Hank both leave.

Cade eyes me for a moment, his gaze fixated on the metal clasp of my overalls. "You should think about it."

"And have you or Jed kill me in my sleep? No thank you." I cross my arms.

He groans as if I'm torturing him. "At least let me take you home since I'm driving to Lake Starlight anyway."

"I can take the boxes. Your dad wouldn't be the wiser."

He grabs a box. "You don't understand how things work in the Greene family. Let's go."

So I grab my purse and follow because I have yet to rent a car—mostly because I didn't want to waste the funds if I wouldn't be setting up shop. But now that I am, I really need to figure out the logistics of a car and a place to live. As good as the apartment sounds, there's no way I can live that close to Cade. My life grew infinitely more complicated when I came here, and getting involved with him would only make it worse.

As we hop in the truck and head toward Lake Starlight, I have to say, I'm a bit afraid of seeing Ethel and Dori again. They apparently tend to get people caught up in things they wouldn't normally do—and Cade is very much one of those things. But I can't deny that the attraction between us is growing no matter how much I try to convince myself I don't like the man.

Chapter Thirteen

"Dodge left."
~ Cade Greene

Cade

I might as well just add up all the people who are in on trying to get me together with Presley Knight. My dad must be one of them since he's offering up the apartment over the garage.

Nikki tried to stay there when she first returned from college, but quickly moved in with the girls. She didn't like being alone in the apartment since our house is set deep in the woods.

"We get in and we get out," I tell Presley when we pull into the Northern Lights parking lot.

I never should've touched the metal clasp on her overalls, but the visual of them falling to the floor and me finding out what color her panties are was nearly unbearable. I expected her to smack my hand away, but she didn't. The entire ride from Sunrise Bay to Lake Starlight, all I could think about was what it means that she let my hand stay on that metal clasp.

"Sounds like a plan." She gets out of the truck.

I pick up a box of fabric and she picks up the spools of thread.

"You're pretty strong for a girl," I joke. My sisters would kick me in the nuts for saying that, but it's clear from everything else that comes out of my mouth in front of Presley, I like to antagonize her, just like I do them. Although there's nothing sisterly about my thoughts when it comes to Presley.

"Say it again and see if you have any balls left." She laughs and walks in front of me, torturing me with the view of her ass.

"Noted."

We enter the retirement community and I realize our first mistake. It's game night and they're all set up in the main area. Even if we put the boxes in front of our faces, there's no dodging everyone. I once got stuck here on Mahjong night and I embarrassingly lost four times to a little Asian grandma who pointed at me after it was over and said, "Suck that."

"Dodge left," I say, and duck down a hallway.

But Presley's not fast enough. Mostly because she probably doesn't think she has to try to outrun these elderly people, but she underestimates how fast they are in the walkers with tennis balls on the bottom. They just slide on by you.

"Presley!"

I close my eyes, crouching behind the wall, when I hear my grandma's voice. Presley, still in the open, looks at me with wide eyes.

"Hank told me you and Cade were going to be dropping off some things. Come and play," Grandma calls.

Presley's smart though and she stays in place.

"Where's Cade?" My grandma's voice grows closer. It's a lost cause. She's going to find me.

"Right here." I come out of hiding around the corner and step up behind Presley. "I hope you like board games," I whisper to her.

"Huh?" she says, but she'll find out soon enough.

"Come, you two, let's get those boxes in the sewing room, then you can join us for a few rounds." Grandma waves us down a small hallway.

"I don't know if I have time for a game," Presley says, looking to me for help I think, I tried to warn her.

"Hot date?" I ask. Yes, for my own knowledge.

"Yeah, with my bathtub."

Jesus. Did she do that on purpose to make me think of her naked in hot water and bubbles? Her smirk says she did.

"Just put them in here." Grandma opens the door and flicks on the lights for the sewing room.

It looks pretty unused with no scraps of fabric anywhere, no half-done projects hanging out around a sewing machine. In fact, I don't even see spools of thread on top of the sewing machines.

As we set down our boxes, I ask, "Grandma, do you guys use this room?"

"Yes. We just know how to clean up after ourselves. Come on, you two." She waves us out.

I raise my eyebrows at Presley like we just uncovered a scheme, and she rolls her eyes. I lean in close to her as Grandma shuts off the lights and closes the door. "They aren't making baby blankets in there."

"What do you think they're doing? Playing strip poker?"

My entire body jolts at the thought. "Don't play dirty."

She laughs and I stop for a moment in the middle of the hall and stare at her. That might be the first time she's laughed in my presence since the first time I met her at the wake.

She tugs on my sleeve. "Come on. We need to win fast and get out."

"At least we're on the same side this time."

Grandma walks us back into the room. Everyone is in groups of four, but once we step in, the woman who works here and seems to be leading things claps.

"Okay, now that Ethel is back, let's all finish our games and switch it up a little," the employee says cheerfully.

"I really should get back," Presley says to Grandma, but she pats Presley's hand with a smile and ignores her comment.

It's Grandma's way of pretending she can't hear her. Just like the Asian grandma who pretended she didn't speak English until she told me to suck it. Sometimes they use their age as a weapon.

Presley and I wait, not really patiently since we're both huffing and groaning as the games end and the lady who works here directs everyone to open up a big area, moving chairs and what-not around one large group game.

Oh shit. This is not a good sign.

"Grandma," I say, but she walks away from me. "She's trying to manipulate us again," I murmur to Presley.

"Maybe she didn't hear you. You mumbled," she says.

"Okay then." I lean back on the table and cross my arms. "Prepare yourself. You're about to be slingshotted out of your comfort zone."

"What?"

When the organizer—Leann, according to her name tag —claps again because as they all move around, there are a lot of grunts and get out of my ways and ouches.

"Charades everyone!" Leann holds up a basket full of folded up notes.

The group sighs.

"I can't get up," one man says.

"My hip," a woman says.

"You expect me to stand?" another man in a wheelchair asks.

"Sweetie, I know you're new, but we don't do charades or Pictionary!" a woman yells.

Leann's cheeks redden.

"Where did she get her degree?" a man loudly whispers to another. "We're old, half of us are in wheelchairs, and the other half are on their way."

Presley's hand lands on my forearm as her other hand covers her mouth. "I feel horrible. We need to do something."

"Um... like what?"

If she thinks we're gonna come up with some new game, she's mistaken. I played broom soccer one time and got hit in the balls so many times, I'm still worried I can't have kids.

"Hey!" Presley raises her hand, but she looks sheepish as she ducks her head as though she's sorry for interrupting. "I have an idea."

"Please." Leann places the bucket on a stool she set up and steps aside, happy to give the spotlight to Presley.

Presley glances at me, her eyes widening as though she's communicating that she wants me to follow her.

I hold up my hands. "This is your show."

She walks back to me, fists my shirt, and yanks me forward. "It's *your* grandma," she whispers.

Point taken. I let her pull me, and once she sees my feet moving, Presley releases me. We walk in front of the group.

"How about we act them out?" Presley waggles her finger between her and me.

"What?" I whisper-shout and start to walk away, but she grabs me by the back of the shirt, yanking me back. She's a lot stronger than I thought.

"Yes, we can pick the words and we'll separate you into two teams. You guys just have to guess. This way all the work Leann did won't go to waste."

They all kind of just sit there, not one smile.

Tough crowd.

And now Presley looks defeated.

Fucking hell.

"Listen, you're all more than capable of coming up here. This is a nice thing that Presley is offering. I suggest you take her up on it," I say in a stern voice.

There are a few murmured conversations. When no one says anything to agree and one man stands with his cane to leave, Grandma is the one who stands.

"We're all doing this. Now sit down, Isaac. That's my grandson and we're interrupting their evening, so let's play."

Dori woots with her fist in the air.

Presley giggles and looks at me as if she loves my grandma. I mean, the woman is awesome, but she's a little too involved for my liking. I thought all grandparents moved to Florida or Arizona when they got older?

"Okay, great. I'll pick the first one." Presley digs her hand in the bin. She reads it and cringes. She holds up a finger to signal that it's one word.

The elderly people all say one out loud. Thankfully they're playing along.

Presley stands with her legs pressed to one another, her hands together in prayer and her head bowed.

"Praying," one lady says.

Presley shakes her head and thinks for a moment, looking at the timer Leann flipped over. Presley sits on the floor, crosses her legs, rests her arms on her legs with her palms facing up. She closes her eyes.

"Buddha?" a man yells.

"Is she bald with a big belly?" a woman asks.

"Let's be nice," Leann says, trying to keep them in line.

Presley shakes her head, looks at me, then holds up her finger to signify for them to give her a second. She stands and bends forward, her palms on the floor and her ass up in the air, giving all the men a show. Some of their eyes bug out and literal drool falls from the corner of their mouths.

"Doggie style?" one man calls.

Presley looks up in disbelief, mouth dropped open. I bite my lip and my inner cheek. Hell, I'm about to rip out a section of the hair on my arm, trying not to laugh.

"You're such a dirty old man," a woman calls.

"You weren't complaining the other night," he says back.

Presley stands, and I admit I was about to throw my coat over her ass so she's not the visual these men have tonight in bed.

"Downward dog." A woman stands and holds up her phone. "Yoga?"

"We shouldn't use our cell phones to find the answers, but you're correct." Leann puts a mark under Presley's team on the whiteboard.

Though this isn't what I want to be doing, seeing the smile that hasn't left Presley's face makes it worth it. I like her a lot better this way than when she's angry at me.

"Greene," she says, walking by me with a cocky gait.

I pick a piece of paper from the bowl and open it.

Sewing

"How easy is this?" I whisper to Presley.

Pulling a chair over in front of a table, I pretend to cut up fabric and press my foot down on the invisible pedal and run the fabric through a machine. I was in home economics once upon a time. I remember how it works. But everyone sits there and doesn't say a word, so I pretend to unroll a spool of thread and run it through the machine down to the needle.

"Oh, I know this one," a woman shouts.

"Then say it," a man yells back at her.

"Give me a minute." Her eyes scrunch as I rack my brain for a way to communicate it better. "Oh." Her arm flies up.

"You're not in school, Olive, just spit it out," the man who I think is her husband snips. I hope I'm not a cranky old man when I'm older.

"Strip poker!" the woman yells.

I freeze. The entire room falls silent and almost everyone looks in the direction of the woman. I look at Presley and we both crack up. Now I'm really wondering if the sewing room is a cover for them playing strip poker. Do they pretend to undress in order to do measurements if a nurse comes in? God, I need to stop my mind from running away with this.

"No. I'm sorry, that's not it," Leann says.

Midge stands and pushes her dark-rimmed eyeglasses up her nose. "Sewing." She smiles, knowing she got it right.

I point, and Leann puts a mark under my name. I'm not sure anyone wants to address the underground strip poker ring going on at Northern Lights Retirement.

"My turn." Presley walks up to the bucket and plucks out a piece of paper. She purses her lips, thinking about it.

I lean against the table, watching her. I wonder if

Presley knows how beautiful she is. It's not even just that she's a knockout in the looks department, but the fact that she's doing charades in front of a bunch of cranky old people and she's giving it her all. She could've just refused to play and dropped off the thread and fabric and patted me on the back. Then again, she didn't have to put the thread and fabric aside for the retirement center in the first place.

Maybe she is made for small-town life after all. Because that's what we do here, put others' needs in front of our own.

She takes off her bandana and wraps it around her neck. Her blonde hair is pulled back into two braided pigtails. "Can I use Cade?" she asks Leann.

"Go ahead," Leann says.

Presley comes up next to me and shows me the piece of paper. "If you get on all fours and I get on your back, I think they'll get it."

I raise my eyebrows. "With these dirty minds, they aren't going to think this." I point at the piece of paper.

She shrugs as though she doesn't have another choice, so I push off the table and get down on my hands and knees.

"Oh, I like this," a man in the front row says.

Presley swings one leg over my back and sits with her legs hanging off, bouncing up and down as she grabs the collar of my shirt.

"What kind of kinky stuff is your grandson into?" someone asks Grandma.

"Cade, sweetie, what are you doing?" Grandma asks next.

"Is that a sexual position I don't know?" the man who called out doggie style asks, tipping his glasses down as though he needs an extra good look.

Presley's laughing so hard, she slips, and I feel her

falling to my right. Somehow, I catch Presley before her head hits the floor. Her laughter stops when she realizes she's under me, and our eyes lock. My gaze falls to her lips and she licks them.

"*Cade Greene!*" Grandma yells as though I'm five.

And just like Grandma put me in this situation, she drags me out right as things got interesting.

Chapter Fourteen

"Why are you on a date with my brother?"
— Cade Greene

Presley

Two weeks after game night at Northern Lights Retirement Center, I still laugh whenever I think about all those elderly people's dirty minds. Then again, I hope I have one when I'm their age. I haven't laughed that much in a long time.

A flyer slides through my mail drop and I pick it up off the floor Adam installed for me last week. He's a hard worker but pretty quiet, which I guess makes sense given that he's nursing a heavy heartbreak. As for his oldest brother, I'm wondering why he's suddenly disappeared this week—even though I shouldn't care what Cade gets up to.

Reading the piece of paper, I'm happy to see that the committee hasn't selected my company as one of the duos for this month.

Twisted Stem and Fired Up will be teaming up for the duo this next weekend.

Come to Fired Up and paint one of three flowers they've
designed for the night
and then buy a bouquet of the real flowers.

Sounds like fun.

Clara knocks on the window. I unlock the door and she slides in, folding up what looks like the same flyer I was just reading and sticking it in her purse. "Oh, it looks so good, Presley." She walks around and takes it all in.

Clara and I have met for coffee a few times and shared one meal at the diner one morning when Adam was painting and she had an evening shift at the library. A friendship has been slowly forming between us. She didn't want my parents' money, but I gave her no option other than to take it.

We tend to stay away from family talk because that subject still feels awkward between us. She feels guilty for her parents' decision, and I feel guilty for popping up and invading her life. It's a cycle I'm hoping we get through in time.

"I wanted to pop in to see if you wanted to go with me to the duo night?"

"Are you sure?"

She laughs and sits on one of the toadstools I just unwrapped. "I think if people see us together, the gossip might stop. Plus, it's your first duo night and since I kind of talked you into staying here, I want to see you actually enjoy it."

I sit on the other stool. "Thank you. I'd love to go."

"Then it's a date. Except for one thing." She clenches her jaw, and I can see that I'm not going to like what she has to say. "Xavier will be with us." I open my mouth to respond, but she quickly puts up both her hands. "He's really great, and I made him swear not to mention his family, especially Cade."

I laugh. "Okay. Should we invite Adam?" I whisper so he doesn't hear me from the storage room he's dry walling.

She shoots me a look as if I'm crazy.

I roll my eyes. "Just as a friend. I feel bad for him."

Clara nods. "I get it. I doubt he'll even come. Remind me to tell you more about his wife later."

"Okay, I'll ask him, and if he says no, at least we tried, right?"

She stands. Her dark hair is in a high ponytail that falls to the side as she tilts her head and fixes her gaze on me for a moment.

"What?"

She shakes her head. "It's a nice gesture, to invite him."

"Did you think I was a bitch?" I can't help but chuckle.

"Not at all. It's just really nice to think of Adam like that." She reaches out to touch my arm but stops midway as though she isn't sure if she should. "Then it's a date. Oh, I can't wait to see what you think of it. I always have fun at these things." She's more excited than me. "I need to get back to the library. Remind me later that I have some suggestions for the young adult book club." She waves and walks out the door before I have time to respond.

Once she's gone, I venture into the back and find Adam on a chair, staring at the wall, his earbuds in his hand.

"Hey, Adam," I say.

He doesn't look at me.

Then I hear music coming from his earbuds. I pick up one and hear a love song. Oh boy.

"You ever hear that song that just takes you back?" he asks, never looking at me.

"Can I have your phone?" I ask, looking around for it

and not seeing it. This situation is starting to warrant an intervention.

"I lost my virginity to this song."

"Okay, TMI. I don't need to know that. And I don't need the reminder when I hear that song too."

"Lucy was so scared. I made this whole romantic scene that night above my dad's garage. He never knew and we lied to our parents..."

Can I please stick my fingers in my ears? I grab the earbuds out of his hand. "Adam, I know it's hard."

He looks at me squatting next to him.

"Heartbreak is never easy, but you gotta get out there," I say. "Go through the motions at least until time works its magic. Clara was just here, and she asked me to go to duo night. Want to come with us?"

He sits up straighter and nods. "Okay."

"Really?" I ask, surprised I didn't have to talk him into it.

"Yeah, I know you're right. It's just facing the damn townspeople..." He shakes his head. "They give me these looks like I'm ready to shatter."

I sit on the floor, bringing my knees to my chest. "Can I be honest?"

He nods.

"They might look at you like that because it looks like it's true."

He sighs and runs his hand through his hair. "I hate how much I miss her."

I put my hand on his knee and run my palm in circles. "She was really important to you, I get it. You have to mourn the end of your relationship."

He huffs. "First my mom and now Lucy. I barely remember mourning my mom. I was too young."

"You guys were all so young," I say.

"Not Cade. He was twelve and I think he still mourns her every day in his own way."

Not wanting to get into the conversation about his mom, since I have no experience in it, I hand him back the earbuds. "I think from here on out, you need to listen to a different kind of music. Something that won't trigger memories."

"Yeah, I guess I should listen to Motown or some shit," he says and puts his earbuds back in, standing to finish the wall.

SATURDAY COMES and I'm at the store, stocking the small amount of books that have arrived already. I understand now why Hank Greene came so highly recommended —he's done amazingly fast work. It helps that Adam has been at my disposal when he's not working as a forest ranger. I'm still waiting on the majority of my books, the round tables, and some decorative pieces. But I'm confident I can set the opening date for three to four weeks from now.

Adam, Xavier, and Clara knock on the window before entering.

"Hey, Presley." Clara walks in and glances in the box. "All great choices."

"I'm glad to see they meet the librarian's approval," I say, standing to greet them.

Xavier holds out his hand. "We've never officially met. I'm Xavier Greene."

I shake it. Being this close to him, I notice the differences between him and Cade. He's a big guy, just as tall as

Cade but much broader. And fairer. Not quite blond, more of a dark blond or really light brown.

"Xavier plays for the Rebels," Clara says with pride.

"Football," Adam adds.

"I know who the Rebels are," I lie because I don't, but kudos to Xavier for making it pro.

"We all played, but this guy got the best arm." Adam thumbs toward his older brother.

"I like to say I had the better work ethic." Xavier winks, and Clara pats his stomach.

"You should've seen this guy last season. He threw three thousand yards and only one interception." She holds up her finger with a proud smile.

Xavier swings his arm around her shoulders and kisses the top of her head. I'd think they were a couple if I hadn't been told differently. "She's my biggest fan."

Adam rolls his eyes. "Goal is to get zero interceptions."

Xavier unlocks himself from Clara and puts Adam in a headlock. They circle around the room, Xavier at the advantage.

After a few seconds, Clara says, "Come on, you two. I don't want to wait forever."

We walk out of the store and I lock up as Clara tells me what we need to do to experience a business duo night. "First, coffee at The Grind. Either that or grab a beer at Truth or Dare."

We all look at the line at the brewery, and I spot Jed and Cade at the bar through the window. There are so many people in there that I'm shocked.

"Do people come here from other towns?" I ask.

Adam shrugs. "Sometimes. But honestly, Sunrise Bay is larger than it seems. People just don't always congregate in town because they like to hate on the tourists who keep our community thriving." He rolls his eyes.

We grab a coffee from The Grind first. Although I would've preferred a beer, I'm not sure I'm ready for another interaction with Cade. Then we wait in line at Fired Up to paint our pottery and I learn more about how long Xavier and Clara have been friends from Adam, who is pretty chatty for a guy who, up until a few days ago, I thought could give a monk a run for his money on the quiet game.

Finally, we get a table for four. Four white ceramic flowers have been laid beside a bouquet of real flowers. A fancy card advertises Twisted Stem.

"They're so cute," I say, and Clara nods. "I call lily." I snag it from the middle of the table.

"I'll take the daisy," Clara says.

"So we're left with roses? Why are the two men painting roses?" Xavier asks.

"Stop being so gender-biased." Clara elbows him, and he fakes an injury.

We get all the paint on our pallets and study the real flowers in the middle of the table.

"This is relaxing," I say, painting my ceramic flower and listening to the overhead music. Hopefully none of the songs send Adam into a tizzy.

We're halfway through and Xavier and Adam are telling me the story of when Marla and Hank got together when a big body sits down on a stool next to me.

I look over. "Cade! Are you painting?"

His gaze scours the table, but I go back to my project, dipping my brush into the yellow.

"Sure." He snatches a lily from a nearby table and grabs a paintbrush.

"Thought you were tending bar?" Adam asks.

"I'm done. Saw you four and figured I'd join in."

"Where's Jed?" Xavier asks.

"He's still at the bar. You know anything artsy isn't his thing."

They all nod in agreement.

"Why not?" I ask.

Cade groans. "He's stubborn. Just doesn't do shit he doesn't want to."

"Oh, that's sad. I mean, I think you learn a lot from doing shit you wouldn't otherwise do." They all laugh. "What?"

"You swore. You look like the type who wouldn't swear." Clara giggles again.

"Do you guys think I'm some goody-two-shoes?" I guess that's better than bitch though.

"We don't know much about you. Why don't you tell us some stuff?" Xavier asks.

Cade's eyes flash to mine, as though he wants information on me too. I guess it's true that I already know so much about him and he knows nothing about me.

"Not a lot to say. I'm from Connecticut. I graduated from Boston University with a business degree. My dad is an investor and my mom stayed at home. I have no sib—"

Clara and I look at one another.

"I didn't grow up with a sibling, although I have a sister now." I smile at Clara and she returns it.

"I heard she's awesome," Xavier says, and Clara's cheeks grow pink.

"That's about it," I say with a shrug.

"All the bullet points," Cade says. There's something in his voice I'm not sure I understand.

"Yeah," I say in a low voice, concentrating on painting.

Xavier and Clara go up to hand their pieces to Theo, who runs Fired Up, and get sidetracked talking to someone. Adam gets up a few minutes later. I have no idea how they finished so fast.

Cade puts down his pottery piece and my stomach churns since I know he's going to say something to me. "I had a lot of fun the other week, at Northern Lights."

"Yeah? You like hanging out with the older crowd?" I laugh in an attempt to appear like I'm not concerned about what he might say.

"Can you answer a question?" His voice is tight for some reason.

"Depends." I continue to work on my ceramic, not wanting to meet the intensity of his eyes.

"Why are you on a date with my brother?"

I glance over, blinking. Surely he's not jealous of his brother who is technically still married to a woman he's clearly still in love with? Not to mention—why would Cade be jealous of *anyone*?

"I'm not on a date. I asked Adam along to get him out of the house and interacting with people. He seemed like he could use it."

Cade stares at me for a moment then eyes my piece of pottery. I continue painting, self-conscious since he's staring at me so intently. I put my paintbrush in the water and hold my ceramic to the real flower to see if it resembles it at all, and I imagine Cade takes the lily from my hand, then grabs my free hand and tugs me up from the chair.

"What are you doing?" I ask as he leads us over to where you hand in your work to be fired in the kiln.

"Theo, this is Presley from The Story Shop," Cade says to the man with a beard.

"I meant to introduce myself earlier—" He holds out his hand, but Cade pulls me away.

"Later, Theo."

"What about Adam?" I ask.

"He's a big boy."

Cade walks us past the crowds of people talking and drinking. A few women have flowers in their hair, holding bags labeled Fired Up. They must've purchased some of the already made items. The next thing I know, we're in a parking lot and I'm pressed up against a truck. Cade unlocks it and opens the passenger door for me to get in.

"I'm a little scared. Are you kidnapping me?"

"No, but I want to be somewhere I know people aren't listening."

"Why?" I ask, but he nudges me in and shuts the door.

One second I hear a click of the door and the next his lips are on mine, my face cradled between his hands, and I sink into something I've wanted longer than I care to admit.

Chapter Fifteen

Cade

"Presley? Presley?" I say again. Is she purposely dodging my question by pretending to concentrate on painting? I wave my hand in front of her face. She blinks.

"Sorry," she whispers, looking at me with lust in her eyes.

I like that look way too much. "Where did you go there?"

Her face reddens, but she dodges the question. "What were you saying?"

"I was asking whether you wanted to go for a walk around town?"

She continues to inspect her ceramic flower. "You mean with everyone? I'd hate to leave Adam."

I search the area and find Adam talking to Tanya Gregory from high school. "He's good."

She follows my line of vision. "Okay, let me just turn this in."

She stands, and I follow her over to Theo. He's marking

each piece to make sure he'll give it back to the right person.

"Hey, Theo, this is Presley from the new business moving in next to us, The Story Shop."

Presley glances back at me as though she's surprised I'm introducing her.

"I meant to make my way over there. Welcome." Theo holds out his hand and Presley shakes it.

"I love your shop. I think I could be here every day."

Theo laughs. "Wait until tourist season when we do glass blowing."

Presley's eyes light up. "Oh, I can't imagine how awesome that must be."

I've never wanted to be a glassblower until this very moment.

Theo's the artsy type. Not that there's anything wrong with that. We might have run in different circles back in the day, but there's no arguing the guy isn't crazy talented.

"All the stuff to look forward to now that you're staying," Theo says.

Presley's shoulders falter a little, but she's quick to recover. Something I'm thinking she's done her entire life.

"We should get going. Thanks, Theo." I gesture with my hand for Presley to go in front of me and follow her out the door. "Come on, let's go this way."

I lead her away from the town and the people, wanting to have her alone. With it already dark outside, I guess that might look a little sleazy.

I want her to feel safe around me, so I ask, "Want to walk toward the bay?"

"Sure." She tucks her hands into her pockets.

I step off the curb to cross the street toward the bay area. "Is that hard? Being here and having everyone know your story?"

"You warned me already. What are you trying to get at now?"

"Nothing, just... I've been there. I understand." I could act like I don't know what it's like to have an entire town watching you, but it's happened twice in my lifetime. The difference was, people already knew me. They don't know Presley.

"Your mom?"

I shouldn't be surprised. Of course someone in this town told her about my mom. "When she died, I couldn't go anywhere without feeling like everyone was studying me, you know? Like they were watching and waiting and wondering when we'd grow used to living without her. They'd tell me what a great big brother I was being to Chevelle. And when Marla returned to town and got together with my dad, they were watching us again. But deep down, I always knew the town was just concerned for us because we were one of them. But you're an outsider and them not knowing you personally yet still knowing everything about your situation must make it harder."

She shrugs and stops to look at the dark bay. A few fishing boats are returning to port, and we can't see the mountain range in the distance in the darkness. "It's not so bad. Back home, people are watching you because they're waiting for you to screw up. They want to make sure to keep you down because they think that brings them up. It's not just gossip. They lie. You should've seen when people found out I was adopted. The claws came out about how I wasn't a *real* Knight."

"Seriously?"

She nods. If it affected her then, she's over it now based on the way she's talking about it.

"Rich people can be ruthless. The girls are just..." Her

gaze remains steady on the bay. "That's why I wanted to stay here." She glances at me. "It's nice here. Something I've never experienced. So they gossip about me?" She shrugs. "It's nothing I can't handle. Maybe with time, they won't see me as Denise Harrison's unwanted child, but just see me as Presley."

"That's the good thing about Sunrise Bay. They're always willing to give someone a fresh start."

"I hope so." She sighs. "Should we head back?"

I could stay here all night and listen to her life story, but she's right. If we don't get back up toward the square area, people will talk.

The town is winding down for the night, but we find Clara and Xavier walking down the street with a bouquet of flowers. Ever since Jed brought up Clara liking Xavier, I'm starting to see things between them differently. But they've been so close for so long... maybe when you have a best friend who's the opposite sex, it's a different kind of friendship.

"Where's Adam?" I ask.

"I think the better question is where did you two disappear to?" Clara asks.

"I just needed some fresh air. It was getting hot with all those people in there." Presley's blushing. Jesus, she's going to have to do a better job than that if she wants people to believe there's nothing going on between us.

Clara nods and Xavier rolls his eyes.

"So where is Adam?" Presley asks.

"He went home. Said thank you for dragging him out," Xavier says.

Clara and Presley walk together, and Xavier and I pick up behind them. We shake hands with and wave to people we've known our entire lives as the four of us head back toward the brewery. Most of the people who stop us tell Xavier what a great season he had. He's only twenty-six and I know he hasn't even had his best year yet. He just got off being second string mid-season last year.

Xavier elbows me and nods at Presley. I shake my head and give him a "shut the fuck up" look. I have to tread carefully here. My family knows me, they know my facial expressions, my usual responses, and I'm sure to tip them off if I try to act as though I don't care at all about her. They'll see right through that.

We end up walking into Truth or Dare, Clara and Presley finding a seat at a table. I head behind the bar and grab a pitcher and four glasses, and that's when I find Molly and Jed looking way too friendly on the other side of one of the keg lines.

I clear my throat and Jed stands up straighter. Molly's been a flirt since forever, especially with Jed. I think she might have a crush on him, or maybe that's just her way. Regardless, it made me hesitate to hire her when she came looking for a job.

"What's up?" Jed steps away as Molly pretends she has to go to the back room for something.

"Nothing. You?" I raise an eyebrow.

He chuckles and slaps me on the back. "You worry too much."

"And you don't worry enough."

The amusement on his face falls when he looks at the seating area. "What's she doing here?" His eyes are narrowed and blazing toward Presley.

Again, I remind myself to watch what I say. "She's here with Clara and Xavier. I just met up with them at Fired Up. You know, you should make an appearance at the duo nights so when it's our turn, people reciprocate."

"That's why our partnership works so well. You go so I don't have to."

I grab another glass. "Want to join us?"

"Nah. I'm out actually." He pats me on the back, grabs his jacket from the counter, and doesn't even bother saying goodbye to the group.

Since we're closed now, I flip the lock then bring everything over to the table and sit down to enjoy the rest of the night with Presley. She seems more at ease with Clara around. I'm happy these two are finding some sort of friendship. I really need to stop this inkling inside me that wants more.

My phone rings and I grab it out of my pocket, seeing Jed's name on the screen. "Did you forget something?"

"Might want to tell your date something's going down at Glacier Point. The girl I was headed out to meet just called and said she needs a place to stay because of some ceiling leaks or something."

"Are you serious?"

Lying about a leak would totally be a Jed thing to do to keep me from enjoying my night with Presley since he views her as our nemesis. I know he wants to stop us from growing any closer since he thinks if her business fails, the building will be ours. He's a persistent guy. With tunnel vision sometimes.

"Yeah. She wanted to stay at our place..." His tone indicates he thinks the girl is crazy. "I just called Mandi and got her a room at the B&B. I figured you wouldn't wanna be in the same situation, so you might want to check to make sure Presley's room isn't affected before Mandi books up. I don't wanna come home and see her in your bed, Cade."

Part of me wants to do exactly that just to piss Jed off. He needs to get over his issue with her.

"Thanks for the heads-up." I hang up because I am not arguing with him about this in front of Presley. I shove the phone in my pocket and see the whole table staring at me. "You might want to call Glacier Point, or maybe we need to go over there. Jed said some rooms had some type of ceiling damage and some people have to vacate their rooms."

Presley's jaw drops for a second, then she reaches for her purse.

"I'll drive you," I say.

"We can go too." Clara follows us.

The four of us leave out the back. We climb in my truck and Presley tries dialing the resort, but no one answers, so she tries again.

In the meantime, Clara is searching for any information on social media. "You're probably fine. It says here that the roof leak only affected one floor." She puts her hand on Presley's shoulder, but Presley doesn't seem to take any comfort in the information.

"Does it say which floor?" she asks.

"It doesn't."

When we pull up to the resort, it's organized chaos. The line to pull up to the front entrance is packed as people with luggage carts stream out and pack up their vehicles. I park along the side, out of the way, and Presley gets out of the truck immediately. We all follow her inside, hanging back and watching as she approaches a tall man who seems to know Presley and ushers her over to the side.

"She knows Wyatt Whitmore?" Clara asks.

I've heard rumors about the owner of the resort. Originally from New York, uber-wealthy, met one of Dori Bailey's granddaughters and relocated here. But how does he know Presley so well? Surely he doesn't know every one of his guests.

"Damn, he really is model good-looking," Clara says.

Xavier raises his eyebrows at her.

"What?"

"He's married."

"I can still appreciate a good-looking man." Clara shrugs. Truth is, Clara is such a tomboy and into her books that I've never really heard her talk about a guy before, so I'm a little surprised as well.

Presley's hand runs down Wyatt's arm and she nods. It's a little too close for my comfort. Turning around, she heads back to us and Wyatt heads on to another group of people.

"My room was affected. He's put my stuff in his office. At least two days."

I pick up my phone. "I'll call my sister at the B&B. Better to be closer to Sunrise Bay anyway."

I walk away as Presley and Clara walk toward the front desk where the ever-so-helpful Wyatt Whitmore stored Presley's stuff in his precious office. How gentlemanly of him.

"You have that look again," Xavier says.

"What look?"

"The jealous one. The one you got when Marla first moved to town and you and Jed were vying for the same spot on the football team." He points at me. "You like her."

No shit, dipshit.

"Mandi." Thankfully my stepsister answers, so I ignore Xavier's observation. "Do you have any rooms left?"

"I just gave away my last one. I have to say, being taken away from my latest binge on Netflix was so worth it. I'm sold out and it's not even tourist season." She's so excited, I think she forgot I was calling to get a room. "Oh, but anyway... who needed a room?"

"Presley Knight," I say.

"Sorry. I've got nothing left. Maybe she can stay with Clara."

I doubt Presley wants to go spend the night in a house her birth mom lived in with pictures of Clara plastered everywhere.

"Thanks, Mandi."

I hang up as Presley and Clara come back, loaded down with bags and wheeling suitcases behind them. Xavier's quick to relieve Clara of the weight.

"Mandi's?" Clara asks.

I shake my head. "She's booked. I doubt we're going to find anything this late."

"Want to come home with me?" Clara asks, but we all know the answer.

Presley shakes her head. "I don't think I'm ready for that. I'll just head farther out of town. I'm sure Anchorage has something available."

"That's ridiculous. Come on, you're going home with me." I pick up her bag.

"I can't do that," she says, catching up to me.

"Relax, you'll stay in the apartment above the garage, and if it's bad, you can stay in my bed tonight and I'll take the couch. We'll get the place ready tomorrow."

"But—"

I swivel around to face her. She doesn't have a lot of choices right now. Clara and Xavier walk ahead to give us some privacy. "I know it's not ideal, but at least stay the night. We'll talk in the morning."

I see her lose the fight as her shoulders slump. "One night."

"Of course, just one night."

Can she tell I'm as full of it as I feel?

Chapter Sixteen

"We need some rules."
~Presley Knight

Presley

We drop Xavier and Clara off downtown so Xavier can drive Clara home, leaving me with Cade. I swear this mishap at Glacier Point has put a permanent smile on Cade's face. Like he wants me to stay at his place. I wish I could share his enthusiasm, but I know this will make my feelings toward him even more complicated. I mean, I drifted off into dreamland tonight and imagined him being so jealous that he yanked me out of Fired Up and took me to his truck and kissed me. My cheeks heat up just thinking about it. Add on what happened at the retirement center and the fact that if we hadn't had that audience, maybe we would've kissed and I'm not sure where we're going to stand soon.

Cade drives down a long driveway surrounded by forest, and eventually a house emerges with a detached garage.

Oh boy, here goes nothing.

"I'm going to warn you, the apartment is probably a mess, so I'd prepare yourself to sleep in my bed tonight."

"And you'll sleep where?" I step out of the truck.

"In my bed too," he says with a smirk, so I know he's kidding.

I refrain from squeezing my thighs together when a picture of what that might be like emerges in my mind. I've never had a one-night stand, but I kind of wish I'd gone home with Cade that first time I saw him at the funeral, back when we didn't know who one another were. Then he'd be out of my system and I wouldn't constantly be in a state of want around him.

"Just kidding. Come on." He jogs up the stairs on the outside of the garage, my bags in hand, and uses his key to open the door.

He flips on the lights and we step inside. It's a great space. Everything is contained in one room—a small kitchen along one wall, a bed farther in, and even a love seat and television in the corner. But there are boxes in the middle of the room, no sheets on the mattress, and cobwebs galore.

"I love it. Thank you."

He chuckles and shakes his head. "Yeah, no. I'll get it cleaned out for you, but tonight, you're in my bed."

Will he please stop saying that?

"It's okay." I step in farther. "I can totally get this cleaned up, then go to bed."

"Yeah, nope." He picks up my bags.

"Put them down. This is fine." I inspect the bathroom which I'll be honest, isn't ideal.

"You're being ridiculous. Come on. I was kidding about sleeping in my bed. I'll sleep on the couch."

"No." I go to pull at the suitcase, but he tugs it back. "Cade."

"Presley. I'm not letting you stay here with all the cobwebs and a toilet that probably hasn't been cleaned in years."

"Why not?"

"I don't know, because I'm a nice guy."

"You're nice for just bringing me here."

He blows out a long breath, losing his grip on the suitcase so all the weight flies toward me and I fall down on my ass.

"Shit, I'm sorry," he says, holding his hand out for me.

"It's okay." I take his hand and stand. "Honestly, I'm more than happy here."

"I can't leave you up here. We can come back tomorrow and clean up then. You can put those overalls back on."

I glance at him, my nipples pebbling with just the memory of his hands on those clasps. I should've let him unclasp them because my body was yearning and begging to have his hands on me.

"Always making fun of my overalls." I circle around so I'm not facing him.

"Oh, I'm not making fun. I fucking love those things."

I want to turn and jump him right now. Which definitely settles it—I cannot sleep in his bed tonight. "I think the space is nice and I'm good with cobwebs. It's not too late, so I'll tidy up a bit and then I'll go to bed. I don't want to fight about this, Cade."

He runs his hand through his longer hair and nods. "Fine. I'll go get some cleaning supplies and I'll move the boxes out for you."

Before I can tell him not to, he disappears from the apartment. I look at the boxes and see that they're labeled in black marker. Hank and Laurie. Trophies. Pictures/albums. I shed my jacket and place it on the kitchen counter, figuring all I need to clean is the bathroom and the corners and the bed area.

Cade returns with a caddy of cleaning supplies, a broom, a duster, and a bag.

"My very own Mr. Clean," I say.

"Want to role-play? You put on the overalls and I'll strip off my shirt. We can play a game of you missed a spot."

I laugh, easing the sexual tension in the room. "You first."

He drops everything and his hands grab the hem of his shirt. "Cool. Should I find the overalls or are you going to handle that?"

I laugh, walking over and stopping him from lifting his shirt. The quick glimpse of his treasure trail stirs something inside me.

"Oh, who am I kidding, this is never gonna work," I say, and his head tilts forward. "Did I just say that out loud?"

He nods, his smile growing wider. "What's not going to work?"

"Nothing." I turn away, but he stops me with his hand on my hip and his chest to my back.

"Presley," he whispers.

My name falling from his lips is so seductive it makes me clench my thighs. I'm barely holding back from wrapping my arms around his neck and kissing him. I need to get him out of here.

"The flirting," I say, owning it. "It's a lot."

His hand leaves my hip and he steps back. I miss his touch as much as I missed *Friends* after Netflix removed it. "You don't like it? Shit... I'm sorry."

I swivel around, and his hand is pulling on his neck and he's staring at the floor.

"No." I shake my head, stepping forward. "I do like it. Too much. Hell, I was envisioning you kidnapping me out of Fired Up and taking me to your truck earlier tonight."

"What?" he asks quietly.

I shake my head. "Nothing. Forget I said anything." Damn me and my big mouth.

"I'm confused." He drops his hand from his neck and stares at me.

I bury my head in my hands, ready to finally hash this out but knowing how embarrassing it's going to be. "I like the flirting. I like the fact that you openly want me to wear overalls because you want to take them off me."

"Actually I just want to slide my hand through the opening on the sides." He chuckles.

His hands land on my shoulders and slide around to my back, resulting in me resting my forehead against his chest. It's so strong, and damn this feels nice after going all these weeks without affection from anyone. I never dreamed I'd miss my mom's constant hugs and kisses on the cheek until I came to Alaska and kept my distance from everyone. But being in Cade's arms feels good, too good. It also feels dangerous.

I step back. "But we can't."

"We can."

He presses his lips to mine, and I don't push him away. As though he's worried I'm going to stop the kiss, he slides his tongue through my parted lips and pulls me closer. I open to him, wanting him more than I care about any consequence, at least in this moment.

"I saw red when you walked by the bar with Adam. I'm not a jealous guy," he whispers, his lips moving down my jaw to my neck.

As he kisses me again, I cling to his hair, threading my fingers through his longer strands, wishing it could be this easy and uncomplicated.

He breaks the kiss, looking pained to do it. "I'm sorry."

I giggle because if he only knew how badly I've wanted to know how he kissed. "Okay, care to explain?"

He sits on the edge of the bed and clasps his hands, his forearms resting on his knees. "I didn't like you with Adam."

I laugh. "No, I mean this." I wave a finger between us.

"You let me kiss you," he says, those eyebrows raised in question like he always does. "I thought there was a fifty-fifty shot you were gonna smack me."

"I wasn't going to smack you." I laugh.

"Why?"

"Well, you threw me at first. I had no time to react."

He huffs. "You're seriously going to go with that?"

"What do you want me to say?"

"That you kissed me back because you liked it. Because you want me just as much as I want you."

I guffaw. "I hate you." Lies. All lies.

He stands, putting his hands on my cheeks and staring into my eyes. "Say it again."

I inhale a deep breath and whisper, "I should hate you."

"But you don't."

"I don't, but that doesn't mean we should be kissing either."

But damn it felt good to go where it feels as though my gut is leading me. I forgot what it was like when you don't fight what comes naturally.

"And why exactly is that?" He drops his hands and steps back.

"Come on, Cade, I have so many issues, every man should run away from me. I'm trying to find myself in a town that belonged to my birth parents who gave me up and kept my biological sister. The last thing I need to add on to that mindfuck is making time for a boyfriend and putting his needs in front of mine."

He walks over and glances out the window. He looks lost in thought until he turns around. "You think I don't have my own issues? I do. And I'm not looking for anything serious either. But damn, I can't get you out of my head. I'm beating off to you every night and I'm fucking thirty years old." He throws his hands out to his sides.

There's a desperation in his voice that makes me want to jump into his arms and tell him I'm here to do with what he wants.

"So what's the answer to our little dilemma then?" I ask, really hoping he has one. I don't know how much more of this tension I can take every time I'm around him.

"We could entertain a friends with benefits relationship." He quirks an eyebrow. "Maybe work it out of our systems. Could be we're not even sexually compatible," he says as though he's thought about it before.

"You could have a small dick." I shrug.

"Or you could lay there like a dead fish," he counters.

I shrug because you never know.

"Though I sense the way you rode me like a cowboy at Northern Lights Retirement that I'm probably wrong on that count."

I shrug again, fighting a smile. His idea has its merits. Sexual satisfaction with no emotional entanglement? No further complications to my life. The denial of wanting Cade Greene is slowly becoming unbearable and something is going to give.

"I guess we have our answer then."

A slow grin spreads across his face and he walks back over to me. "Great. It's settled."

I put up my hand and step back. "We need some rules."

"For sure, let's get the rules sorted out."

It's my suggestion, so why is the next thought in my head that rules are made to be broken?

Chapter Seventeen

"I think we have a squatter."
~ Fisher Greene

Cade

She's right. If we don't put down some firm expectations and things to stay away from, we're asking for trouble.

"No one can know," she says.

"You embarrassed to be sleeping with me?"

"No, but if people know, rumors and expectations of marriage and babies won't be far behind."

I nod. "Deal."

"No sleepovers, no restaurants."

"You're a dream come true." I lean forward, my lips begging to touch hers again.

"Do you have any rules?" she asks.

"One," I say, holding up my finger.

"Okay, what is it?"

"Those overalls? You wear them every day."

She laughs and I take the opportunity to move in, knowing I've got permission for my hands to wander where I've imagined them being for weeks.

But she places her hand on my chest and leans back. "First, we have to clean this apartment."

I grab her hand. "Wrong. Tonight you're in my bed, and tomorrow we clean this apartment."

She doesn't fight me, thank fuck. Jed is still out, and Adam is probably asleep already. Fisher's truck isn't here. I can get her into my room without anyone knowing.

"We're moving kind of fast," she says behind me when we hit the stairs.

"I've wanted you for weeks and now you're giving me the green light." Did I seriously just admit that to her? Oh well.

We walk through the back door that opens into the kitchen and we're one step up on the stairs when "My Girl" by the Temptations plays from Adam's room.

"What the hell?" I mutter.

She laughs behind me and I look back at her. "Inside joke between me and Adam."

That doesn't work for me.

I get her in my bedroom and shut the door. "I really don't like you having inside jokes with my brother."

She ignores my comment and looks around my childhood bedroom. I haven't done a whole lot to it. Sure, the shit from high school is all packed away, so I'm not embarrassed by trophies or a prom king sash—with mine and Reese's names on it—hanging from my corkboard. But she picks up a bottle of cologne I borrowed from Jed weeks ago and wiggles her nose, setting it back down.

I come up behind her, pushing her hair to one side, and lean down to kiss her neck. She stills until my lips meet bare skin, then she relaxes under my lips. Her arm snakes behind us and runs along my ass.

"Are you sure this is a good idea?" she says softly.

I spin her around and she wraps her arms around my neck. "Are you kidding me? This is the best idea I've ever had."

She rises on her toes and I bend my neck until our lips meet. How could she deny this? Everything about this feels right when my lips are on hers.

I wrap an arm around her waist and press her to me. My other hand cradles her cheek and I kiss her jawline and down her throat. She moans and I rise up to swallow her moan as if I'm in high school and my dad is about to come up here. But if we're going to keep this secret, we can't be too loud.

I pull away, torturing myself and her, lock the door, and turn on my television. It's on ESPN, not that I give a shit what's on.

Leading her to my bed, I sit on the edge and bring her in front of me, between my legs, then undo the button of her jeans. "This okay?"

Her answer is to grab the hem of her shirt and pull it off, leaving me with the sight of her tits nestled in a dark gray bra. I lower her zipper and push her jeans down her shapely legs. She steps back, kicks off her shoes, then takes off her socks and her jeans, until she's completely naked except for a matching bra and panty set.

"God, you're gorgeous." I lean in and press a kiss to her stomach.

"Your turn," she says, stepping forward.

I kick off my shoes. "Come sit on my lap."

"Are you pretending to be Santa?" she asks.

I chuckle, happy she's not self-conscious about our first time. At least she doesn't appear to be.

"Sure, what do you want for Christmas this year, young

lady?" I am somehow able to get the words out without laughing.

"A lollipop?" She bursts out laughing.

"Only if you're able to lick it all," I say.

She's shaking her head, her forehead falling to my shoulder. "I can't."

I grab her chin with my finger and thumb and press my lips to hers. Her arms wrap around my neck and my fingers graze up her inner thigh before massaging her clit through her panties. She leans back and releases a breathy sigh.

My fingers wrap around the edge of her wet panties and I slide the fabric over.

Bang. Bang. Bang.

Her head snaps up as though getting caught means we'd go to jail rather than just be outed by one of my brothers.

"Cade!" Fisher screams.

"Give me a second," I say to Presley, trying to keep my frustration in check.

She scrambles off my lap to grab her clothes.

If I had to trust any brother with my secret, it would be Fisher, but since I don't think Presley has ever met him, it's probably not a good time. I lower the volume on my television, unlock the door, and slide out.

Fisher's standing in the hallway, and he turns on the hallway light as though he's about to interrogate me.

"What?"

"Who's in there?" he asks and crosses his arms.

"None of your business."

"Whatever. I don't give two shits who you fuck. But we have a problem."

"What is it?"

"Ain't No Mountain High Enough" by Marvin Gaye plays from Adam's room.

"What the hell is that?" Fisher asks.

"I have no idea. It's been Motown all night."

"And let me guess, it got you and your lady friend all horny?"

"Lady friend? Has all that ink from Smokin' Guns finally poisoned your brain?"

Most of us have tattoos, but Fisher's taken it to another level. I'm not saying they aren't cool. Liam at Smokin' Guns in Lake Starlight does a bang-up job, but when you look at Fisher's upper body, you'd never guess the guy was the sheriff of Sunrise Bay.

Fisher waves me off. "The lights above the garage are on, so I went up there to investigate. I think we have a squatter."

"Yeah, I know who the squatter is. It's fine." I turn and put my hand on the doorknob to go back into my room.

"Well, she has sexy lingerie."

I spin back around. "You searched her belongings?" I ask a little too loudly.

I hear Presley screech through the door.

"I'm a sheriff. I'm not gonna just run down the stairs scared. I investigate shit."

I shake my head. "Well, no worries, dad's letting someone stay there temporarily."

"Who?" he asks, widening his stance and recrossing his arms.

"None of your business."

"I'm gonna find out," he says. "Just tell me."

My door opens and Presley steps out next to me. "Hi. I'm the squatter. And I really hope you aren't one of those guys who likes to wear women's panties."

Fisher looks her up and down. "Story girl?"

"If you're asking if I'm the woman who's opening The Story Shop? Yes, that's me."

"This is my brother, Fisher. Sheriff Greene if you want to be formal, which none of us ever are," I introduce the two. "Fisher, this is Presley Knight."

They shake hands.

"Nice to meet you," she says.

He takes in the two of us next to each other. I'm sure Presley's messy hair and both of our swollen lips are dead giveaways as to what we were doing.

"I should get back and clean up." She ducks around us.

"No worries," he says and she stops at the top of the stairs. When she doesn't respond, Fisher finishes. "I don't wear women's panties unless it's her kink." He winks and she laughs, then heads down the stairs.

After we hear the back door close, my gaze falls to Fisher. "This is a secret. No telling anyone. Especially Jed."

He holds up his hands. "That's your business. She's cute though. Might want to make sure she's satisfied before another Greene slides his way in there."

I know he's egging me on, but still. "You might be the sheriff, but I'm the oldest."

"That doesn't hold weight anymore, old man," he says, but I'm already walking down the steps.

So much for us keeping this between us. Five minutes in and one of my brothers already knows.

When I reach the apartment, Presley is already in the bathroom, scrubbing it down. Instead of bothering her, I use the duster in the corners, sweep the floor, and move the boxes to the unfinished part on the other side of the garage. Since she's still in the bathroom when I finish all that, I put some sheets on the bed and head back inside to grab an extra pillow, blanket, and towels. I don't really want to give her the ones we use when our drunk friends spend the night, so I give her mine. I'll use the designated drunk blanket and pillow tonight. Since Marla stocks our toiletries because of her coupon obsession, I pull shampoo, conditioner, and soap out of our closet.

I somehow get all this accomplished before she's done in the bathroom, so I poke my head in there. "All good now."

She stops and walks out into the main room and looks around. "You did all this? I'm impressed. Who did you learn to clean from?"

"My mom."

Her smile drops and she grabs her suitcase, putting it on a chair in the corner. "Well, she did a great job. I was expecting to be up all night."

I sit on the bed. "So my brother knows."

She nods, pulling out some clothes. "Obviously. Will he tell anyone?"

"I don't think so."

"I think I'm going to take a shower." She nods toward the bathroom door.

I guess that means sex is off the table for tonight. *Thanks, Fisher.*

"Okay, I'll get out of your way then." I stand, and she hesitates.

"Stay," she says. "I mean, unless you don't want to."

I place my hands on her hips. "I'd love to stay. Do you need help washing your hair?"

She bites her lip. "This is going to sound crazy, but I'm not sure I'm ready for you to..." She stops and inhales a deep breath. "Yeah, I'd love help."

Whatever changed her mind, I'm not going to wait for her to change it back. I take the hem of her shirt and slowly raise it up her body until it's over her head and on the floor at our feet.

When I reach around to find her bra strap, she laughs. "It's in the front."

I unclasp it in the front and the weight of her tits pulls the fabric apart. I gently peel the cups off her breasts and slide the straps down her arms, sucking in a breath while my dick presses even harder against the zipper of my jeans. She's absolute perfection.

Her jeans are next, and I shed them off her body as quickly as possible. I kind of want to keep her in her panties because this look right now is sexy as hell, but I slide those down her legs too, squatting as I go, leaving me on my knees in front of her. I stare up at her and take my chance, sliding my finger along her folds. She bucks toward me, chasing her pleasure, and I lean forward and switch out my fingers for my tongue.

"Cade," she says, "I should shower."

She's crazy. I've waited this long, and now that I've had a taste of her, I'm not stopping until I get my fill. There's no more time to be wasted until she's mine. I turn us around so she sits on the edge of the bed, facing me, and put one of her legs over my shoulder.

I've got all night and no one else knows we're up here. We can be as loud as we want. I can't wait to hear the sounds that come out of her once I'm buried deep inside her.

Chapter Eighteen

Presley

Cade lifts my leg, his lips pressing featherlight kisses along my inner thigh until he positions it over his shoulder. Then he's front and center with my pussy. Thank God for the Glacier Point spa's waxing services. Of course, I've been on my hands and knees, cleaning the bathroom. But Cade strips away all my inhibitions when he nibbles right where my thigh meets my center.

The anticipation of his mouth on my clit makes my back fall to the mattress, unable to watch it actually happen. As soon as his tongue strokes up my folds and twirls around my clit, pleasure wraps me in its warm embrace. His touch is soft and leaves me wanting more, so I grind my core to his mouth for more friction.

He takes a break, and I rise on my elbows. His heated eyes are glued on me. "Good?"

"Yeah," I say breathlessly.

He dips his head back down between my thighs, and

this time, I can't stop watching him. We both groan and moan as he licks and sucks me. It's been way too long since I've had a guy's mouth on me, and I'm not prepared when the intense tingling pulses through me. He grabs my hips, tugging me closer, so my ass hangs off the bed. I grip the long strands of his hair with one hand, making sure he has no plans of stopping, while I shamelessly buck along his face. His groan grows louder and fills the small room.

He grips my ass as though he's saying that I'm not going anywhere until I'm a fumbling mess. God, if he's this good at oral, I can't imagine the magic he can create with his dick. One of his hands disappears from my ass, and a second later, his finger teases my opening.

I have no energy to watch him anymore, and my back falls to the bed as waves build on top of one another. Then he adds a second finger and those waves build to a tsunami. In and out his fingers move masterfully, building my orgasm. His mouth covers my clit, working in the perfect pattern. I clench hard on his fingers, trying to stave off my climax and enjoy this for a few more minutes.

But the strangled noise that leaves him as though he's tortured by the thought of what that will feel like around his dick sends that giant wave crashing on the shore and undoes me as I spiral into pure bliss. No worries, no second-guessing, just me filtering like water onto a sandy beach until I'm limp on the bed, sprawled out for his viewing pleasure.

He kisses his way up my body. I want to lie here and enjoy it, but he's got way too many clothes on. So I flip him over.

"I take it that was a winner?" he asks, a sly grin in place. "I mean, to keep up my end of the arrangement?"

"Do you need an ego boost, Cade?"

His fingers land on my ribs, tickling me until I'm the one on my back.

"Your screams were enough," he whispers, kneeling in front of me, then he strips off his T-shirt with one hand behind his back. I don't know why it's sexy as hell when guys do that, but it is.

I slide my hands down his chest. The man is incredible, lean muscle from his biceps to his rippling abs.

"Don't worry, you can wash your panties afterward."

I shove his chest. "Cocky much?"

He grabs my hands and puts them on his jeans where I can feel his straining erection under the denim. "With you? Never."

The moment grows serious somehow. I have no idea how he's able to switch gears so fast.

I unbutton his jeans and slide down the zipper. With his help, he's out of his jeans, only in his boxer briefs. I've always loved the power of making a man rock-hard. His smoldering eyes watching my hand rub along his stiff length gets me wetter.

He puts his hand over mine, applying more pressure, and our eyes lock. "Damn, your hand feels too good on me."

I slide it under the waistband of his boxers. He's the perfect mix of silky soft over hard strength, pulsing in my hand.

"Fuck," he murmurs when I move my hand up and down.

He hooks his fingers under his waistband and pushes them down his hips, so I don't have to take my hand off of him. And he's a sight. My experience in the sex department is minimal. Enough to know what a guy likes, but not enough to feel like a master. So I appreciate that he was comfortable enough to show me how much pressure to use. I tighten my grip and pump him, and he touches my breast, thumbing my nipple.

"I have really bad news," he says, his voice strained.

"Am I doing it wrong?" How embarrassing is this?

"Jesus, no." His large hand never leaves my breast. "I'm assuming you don't have condoms."

Fuck, he's so right. "Why do you assume that?"

His eyes light up. "You do?"

My head falls back on the mattress. "No. I don't."

Still, I pump him because although I want to know what he feels like inside me, I'm not opposed to returning the favor of an orgasm.

"I have them in my room, but in order for me to get them, we have to stop doing what we're doing and I have to get dressed."

I raise up on my knees and his hand falls from my breast. Once I'm on my knees, staring at him with the tip of his dick in front of my mouth, he uses both hands to reach around me and grab my breasts.

"Then let me repay the favor."

"I really want to fuck you though," he says.

But he loses the fight when I put my mouth on him. My tongue slowly licks up him until precum glistens on his tip. I twirl it with my tongue and wrap my mouth around him. He bucks forward.

"Damn," he says in a rough voice.

I push him down my throat and raise back up, pumping with my hand at the base because I'm not sure I can fit all of him in my mouth. His noises become uncontrolled and my own arousal peaks again. When I continue working him, his hands slide into my hair and he pumps into my mouth a few times before he eases out of me and slides off the bed.

"Sorry, I need to be inside you. Give me a second." He shrugs off his jeans and stares at me naked on the bed. "Don't move."

He points at me and runs out of the apartment. Seconds later, I hear tires on the gravel and Cade runs back into the apartment and shuts off the lights.

"It's Jed," he whispers and I feel him settle beside me. "I guess no sex tonight unless we want *two* of my brothers to find out."

I take his long, thick length in my hand and shimmy down the bed.

"I hate not seeing you, but damn, your mouth should get an award." His fingers grip my hair and he tugs lightly, making me want to please him more, to get the nonverbal reactions of how much he's enjoying my mouth on him. I use what I thought were mediocre blow job skills, but Cade acts as if I'm a porn star, gripping my hair tighter while his hips buck off the bed.

"I'm gonna come."

I don't stop even after his warning. I'll swallow him down. He must understand because a second later, a noise pours out of him that's so arousing, I'm ready to tell him I have an IUD and I'm clean so let's just have sex.

He pumps into my mouth once more and stills, pouring into the back of my throat. I lick him clean and make my way up his body, straddling him. His hands manipulate my tits and he urges me to lower down a bit.

"I need my mouth on these."

His mouth covers my nipple and his fingers pinch my other one. He spends time worshiping my breasts, not that I'm complaining. I love my breasts being played with, and as he shifts from one to the other, I'm already there, ready for my next orgasm as though Cade is giving them out like

Halloween treats and I'm shamelessly coming back for seconds.

He reads me perfectly and moves one hand between my legs, his thumb putting a small amount of pressure on my clit. I don't sit up because his mouth shifts again to the other nipple. He's going to make me come just like this. You'd think Cade was familiar with me already, that this wasn't our first but our fiftieth time in this position with the way he plays my body to perfection.

I groan when his teeth scrape along my nipple and he increases the pressure on my clit. That's all it takes for the pulsing waves to crash to shore with hurricane force and I cry out. I collapse on him and he holds me, his calloused palms running down the length of my back. Up and down in a steady rhythm.

He kisses my cheeks and neck. "You're stunning when you come."

I exhale, my heart still pounding. "Imagine when you're inside of me."

His dick twitches between my legs.

"I'm hoping if you're happy with my performance that we can repeat this with a box of condoms tomorrow night."

I rise up on my hands. "Tomorrow, huh?"

"Well, you're not out of my system by a long shot."

His words make my cheeks blush and my heart flutter. But the truth is, he's not out of my system either. If anything, I'm more intrigued to find out what other things he's mastered in the bedroom.

I should've known that one time with him wouldn't be enough to satisfy me. Maybe once we actually have sex, I'll be done with him and able to get him out of my head.

"Now we shower." He kisses my temple, slides out from under me, and I hear the shower start.

Yeah, I'm good in bed. I slide under the sheets and nuzzle into the pillow that smells like Cade. Not the cologne that was in his room, but him, the scent of his skin and of his clothes. My eyes drift closed with a satisfied sigh.

Chapter Nineteen

"Goldilocks is sleeping in someone else's bed."
– Nikki Greene

Cade

After I left Presley asleep in her bed last night, I dressed and locked the door behind me. Since this is my first time ever entertaining this type of relationship, I figure it's better to stick to the rules even if I felt like shit leaving without saying anything to her.

Jed comes into the kitchen through the back door after his run. I thought he was in bed still. Here I am with two bagels and two yogurts I was about to take outside.

"I hear we have a guest?" Jed glances at the tray and shakes his head. "What are you doing?"

"I'm not going to let her starve."

"You're a better man than me." He opens the fridge and takes out his green juice smoothie.

I set down the tray, figuring we should hammer this out now. Especially since I'm starting... whatever this is with her. I don't want the guilt that Jed doesn't like her hanging over my head while I'm on the cusp of an orgasm. "Okay, her store is practically ready to go. You can stop with the grudge now."

He sits at the table and bends to untie his shoes. For a moment, I think he's going to ignore me. But he straightens, toes out of his shoes, and meets my gaze. "You think I don't know you want her? Hell, you wear your emotions more than the mother of a newborn who cries at every commercial."

"How I feel isn't the topic of conversation."

"I don't hate her. I'm still pissed about the building though. I wanted it for us. And we almost had it."

Jed is a complicated guy. He grew up in the lap of luxury back in Arizona, his daddy buying everything for him. He's made huge strides so that he's not that guy who expects things to always go his way, but he can't seem to stop with this one. It's over, we lost the opportunity to expand the building, and all we can hope is that Ginny from the doll shop on the other side of us decides to retire soon and doesn't have some long-lost daughter to will it to.

"I get that you're disappointed, but it's not her fault. Plus, imagine what she's going through."

He shakes his head. "You're such a softy. Always have been. Look what happened with Reese."

As if I really want to talk about my high school girl-friend right now. "Just give Presley a chance. I think she'll surprise you. Adam really likes her."

Speaking of, Adam enters the room with his AirPods in. He's singing "Please Mr. Postman" by The Marvelettes. Jed shakes his head at him.

At least Adam's in a better mood than before.

"Fine." Jed points at me. "I'll give her a chance, but I'm not making any promises."

I chuckle. "Okay, good enough." I pick up the tray. "I'm taking these up to her."

"Try not to let your dick accidentally slide into her while you're up there."

I stop short at the door, then walk through it, not wanting to get into it with him. I just hope Fisher keeps his mouth shut.

I knock when I reach the top of the stairs, and Presley answers. She's wearing another pair of tight jeans and a long-sleeve T-shirt.

"'Morning," she says. If she's upset I left last night, she's not showing any signs of it.

"I knew you didn't have anything here." I hold the tray a little higher.

She nods. "Thank you."

I place the tray on the counter, and she goes back to putting on her makeup in the bathroom.

I stare at her reflection through the mirror and work up the nerve to say what I came up here to say. "I think you should stay here longer than you originally intended."

She stops mid-stroke with her blush brush but starts back up again. "Listen, I had a great time last night and I'm all for continuing that, but me staying here is just going to complicate things."

"Why? If anything, it gives us more opportunity to do what we want to be doing." I wrap my arms around her waist and kiss her neck.

"Because of this. I'm not sure our arrangement should include you bringing me breakfast. I actually think our arrangement ends much like it did last night. After we're satisfied, the other party leaves. Anything to do with morning is usually off-limits." She swivels in my arms, and since she's yet to put on lipstick, I kiss her, my tongue sliding into her mouth. Her breath is minty as though she just finished brushing her teeth.

The minute our kiss deepens, her arms wrap around my neck and I grab her ass, spurring her to straddle me as I prop her up on the counter. Damn, I wanted to be inside her last night. My morning wood wasn't nearly satisfied with my palm. It wanted Presley wrapped around it tight.

"Hey, guys!" Adam yells, knocking *after* he announces himself.

We dislodge so fast you'd think we're world-class sprinters. I fall to my knees as though I'm looking at something, and one glance at Presley and I see that she looks as if she's wearing too much blush.

"Hey, Adam." She leaves the bathroom first.

I follow. "I was fixing the toilet. Something's up with it. Keeps running."

Adam seemed okay minutes ago, but he's got that depressed expression again as he takes in the apartment. "Looks nice up here."

Presley's hand runs down his arm as she passes him and she picks up half the bagel I made for her, biting into it. What have I missed? I'm used to being jealous of Jed from time to time, but I've never had to be jealous of my youngest brother.

"What did you need?" I ask Adam, grabbing a yogurt on the tray.

"I thought you could drive me today since I'm at the store."

I had plans of driving Presley and maybe pulling over outside the city limits for a quick make-out session. At the very least, I had high hopes it wasn't Adam's day to help at the store and I could sneak over and we'd christen The Story Shop. But I suppose that's not happening now.

"Sure."

"Don't sound too excited." He pats me on the back. "Just grab me when you two are ready."

He jogs down the stairs and I watch him go. How is he not in the anger stage of his grieving yet?

"You can drop me off at the rental car place. It's about time I get a car," Presley says.

"I can take you back and forth."

Her shoulders falter. "No, you can't, and I'm not staying here long-term either."

She's so damn stubborn.

"Fine, I'll take you after work. And we can hit up the grocery store too." I finish my yogurt and throw it away.

"You really are pushy, you know that?"

"And you're hot." I corner her and place my hands on her hips, thankful we came to this arrangement that gives me permission to touch her. Although I'm quickly becoming addicted to having her lips on me and my hands on her.

She gives me a chaste kiss. "Come on, we should go."

She abandons the rest of the food. I grab my bagel, tossing everything else in the trash. I follow her down the stairs of the apartment, wishing we were climbing the stairs instead because I'm about to spend my entire workday with a raging hard-on.

IT'S lunchtime before I get a break from phone calls and handling the end-of-the-month paperwork. Jed is out on site visits to some of the places that carry our beer. I'm happy for the alone time since he hates paperwork and just complains the entire time. Easier for me to do it myself.

A replay of Nikki's segment from earlier today comes on the radio and I groan. Part of me wants to turn it off, but the other half of me wants to make sure she's not talking about me. Or Presley.

"You know what I hate about living in the same town as my siblings?" she says to her co-host, Chip. Chip's in his fifties but seems more interested than he should be in the gossip she spews out. She doesn't even wait for him to answer. "I hate hearing about their sexual escapades. It makes me imagine them." She makes a gagging sound into the mic.

"What hot news do you have for us today?" Chip asks.

"My stepbrother, Cade Greene, has been seen multiple times with Sunrise Bay's newest resident, Presley Knight. Knowing Cade the way I do, I'd say he's smitten. Especially when it was reported they were at the bay last night and a little birdie from one town over in Lake Starlight told me that Miss Knight had to check out of Glacier Point Resort due to a water leak. I'm sure none of us are surprised that my brother, Cade, rescued her and she's now staying above the garage at his house."

"Didn't you stay there for a while?" Chip asks.

I should write him a thank you note for changing the subject.

"I did, and let me tell you, no woman would want to stay there, so I have my own theory that Goldilocks is sleeping in someone else's bed."

"Which bear's bed do you think she's in?" I have no idea how Nikki's partner-in-crime plays along as though they have a script. Hell, maybe they do. I don't know.

"Not the Ranger Bear or the Sheriff Bear. We all know the Charismatic Bear is wondering why he hasn't scored with her, but I'm willing to bet the Gentleman Bear is the one getting Goldilocks's honey."

Chip laughs and I roll my eyes. She's insane, but I can't deny her ratings are big because of this shit.

"I haven't seen my brother so enamored since he was with Reese and that was back in high school. So why don't we play a song that fits the happy couple perfectly?"

"I can't wait," Chip says.

"This is 'Perfect Strangers' by Jonas Blue. Enjoy, everyone," she says, and the song plays.

I turn off the radio and go through the back door over to Presley's store. Adam is in the storage room, stocking boxes, and I catch Presley out front, trying to put up the awning herself.

"What the hell are you doing?" I say to Adam. "Why is she on a ladder?"

I run through the store and out the front. She's inching up on her tiptoes to pull down the upper part.

"Why on Earth are you trying to do this yourself?" I demand.

"What? I'm fine." But she loses her footing when she looks down at me and I catch her in my arms.

Adam comes out of the store. "She didn't tell me she was doing it."

"Because you've got music in your ears twenty-four hours a day," I yell. He's gotta get out of this funk and back in the world of the living.

Presley wiggles out of my hold and I realize I'm holding her as if she's my bride and we're about to walk over the threshold. Chuck comes out of the butcher shop, blood-stains on his white apron, to see the commotion. His bushy eyebrows rise when he sees me, and a customer whispers something in Chuck's ear while walking past him into his shop. Luckily, Chuck follows her in. I'm in no mood to hear his sarcastic comments.

"I would've helped if she'd told me. I was stocking the storage area," Adam argues.

"Exactly my point." I put Presley down because if I don't, she's going to fall with the amount of wiggling she's doing in my arms.

"Just stop, both of you. I can do things on my own."

Here we go again, her proving a point.

"You should at least have someone spot you," I say in a loud voice, grabbing the attention of two middle-aged women walking out of The Grind.

"Just relax," Presley says in a hushed voice. "Is the segment just moments ago not enough?"

So she heard it.

"Nikki's up to her usual tricks?" Adam asks, putting his AirPods back in and walking into the store.

I throw up my hands.

"I can do things myself without you yelling at your poor brother for not helping me."

I stuff my hands in my pockets. "What is with you and my brother anyway?"

She stares blankly at me. "Seriously? Your brother?"

"What's that supposed to mean?" I ask.

"You're jealous of your brother." She leans in close and whispers, "I don't think it was his mouth between my legs last night."

Just the memory of her taste makes me want to take her over my shoulder and carry her into the Truth or Dare office. If only I had condoms at the brewery. Which reminds me, I need to carry one around with me as if I'm sixteen again and believe the false notion that the opportunity for sex is always around the corner.

"Come, let me feed you lunch, then we'll finish the awning." I grab her hand and she actually lets me take her over to the brewery.

"Are you going to feed me a hot dog?" She laughs, our fight over, I suppose.

I open the doors of the brewery with my keys in my pocket, lead her in, and lock it back up. "Come on now. You know it's a Kielbasa sausage."

She laughs, but my hands are busy roaming up the hem of her T-shirt as I guide us to my office. Just as I have her ass on my desk and my hands on her tits, I hear the back door open then Jed humming as he turns the doorknob to the office.

Presley

I lean over Cade's shoulder, pretending I'm looking at something he's showing me on the computer.

"See," Cade says, pointing at a blank cell on an Excel spreadsheet.

"Oh, I get it."

Jed walks in and stops in his tracks, taking in our positions. "Figures you two would get all hot over numbers." He rounds Cade's desk, never looking at the screen before plopping down in his chair.

If he only knew that Cade's dick is very hard under this desk because moments ago, his hands were on my breasts. I'd very much like them there again. His whole heroic act of saving me while I was doing the awning shouldn't turn me on, but call me a damsel because it kind of warmed me that he was protective.

"I'm starved. Want me to make you something in the kitchen?" Cade asks.

Since Jed's presence never sits well with me, I agree. I

pull out my phone. "I'm just going to text Adam and ask him to pull the ladder in."

Jed stands. "I'll tell him. I have a date I wanna set him up on, and since you two are doing whatever you're gonna do, I'm out. Don't dirty up the kitchen before service tonight." I'm pretty sure he doesn't mean dirty the dishes. "I'll be back."

Music to my ears. Jed walks out of the office and we hear the door slam behind him.

I straddle Cade's lap, grinding along his hard bulge. "About that Kielbasa?"

"It's hot and ready."

I'm pretty sure my cheeks are fire-engine red. His hand slides around my neck and brings my mouth to his. Not taking any time, his tongue glides through my lips and mingles with mine. He really is a great kisser. Not too aggressive, but far from passive. My hips move on their own accord, chasing the pleasure Cade elicits.

His hands lift the hem of my shirt, only stripping his lips off of me to see me in my bra. His fingers go to the front, but this bra clasp is in the back.

"I'd like to request front clasps from here on out." He pulls down the cups and bends me back, taking a breast into his mouth before I can respond.

My arms anchor around his neck and he bucks his hips off the chair, aligning perfectly with my core. The only problem is we're both wearing jeans and they don't allow it to feel as satisfying as I wish it was. But his mouth devouring my breasts feels amazing. His tongue twirls, his mouth sucks, and he blows a stream of air on my nipples, causing them to harden even more.

"Can I just stay here all day?" he murmurs against my breast.

"No complaints here."

He stands from the chair and rests my back on his desk. The stapler presses into my right shoulder blade, but that's a small price to pay. He unbuttons my jeans and lowers my zipper, his eyes promising me that I'm going to love every second of what's about to happen. I have no doubt.

His large palm slides down the front of my pants, past the threshold of my panties, and his long finger slides through my folds before concentrating on my clit. He has a black belt in clit mastery—I swear he plays me almost better than I can myself.

Wanting to touch him, I straighten up and unbutton his jeans. I pull them open as much as possible, and my hand rubs his hard length through his boxers.

God, I feel as if we're in high school with all this foreplay and getting each other off with our hands and mouths. I kind of like it, rather than going straight to sex, although I'm sure I wouldn't be complaining if he was deep inside me right now.

Just his lips all over my skin and the pressure of his palm on my clit and his finger teasing my entrance is enough to get me there. Mostly because the dark stubble on his cheeks along my breast is a torture of the best kind. Right in his office, I come undone and a shiver runs up my spine like the last sizzle of a spent firecracker after the grand finale.

When I come to, he's staring at me and places one kiss at my navel. "I could watch you come every minute of the day."

He slides me forward and I'm very aware he's still hard. I slide onto his lap and give him a quick kiss. His hard-as-steel dick is between us.

When I move to slide off his lap and down to the floor, he stops me. "I need to get inside of you."

"Are you refusing a blow job?"

"Hell no. But I'm not going to be satisfied until I sink into you."

Just thinking about it gets me going again.

"Well, unless you have a condom in that drawer..." I hate the fact I haven't told him we're probably good to go bare, but I'm not ready to go there yet.

"I think it speaks to how clean I am that I don't."

I lower myself to the floor, bringing his jeans and boxers down farther on his hips. Once I lick up his length, his head falls back. And soon we're exactly where we were yesterday, his hand in my hair while he comes down my throat. After we're done, his thumb runs along my bottom lip and he stares in my eyes as if I'm a puzzle he needs to figure out.

"You're way too good at that," he says, but I feel as though there's something else he wanted to say. Something he's holding back. Especially when he urges me up under my arms and wraps his arms around me, kissing my neck. "I wish we could take a nap."

Last I knew, friends with benefits don't take naps, so I spring back. "I'm really hungry."

"You're not full enough after the Kielbasa?" He taps my ass to get up off him.

We both button our pants and I put myself back together, finger-combing my hair, and we head to the kitchen where he prepares me a sandwich.

"So the rental place has a car for me. You can drop me off, then I'm heading to the grocery store."

"And what about staying there for a while longer?"

I've been thinking about it all morning. Being at the apartment this morning was nice. It's not much bigger than my room at Glacier Point, but it'd be cheaper. Plus it has a kitchen, and it would be nice to cook for myself a little. "I want to pay rent."

He shakes his head.

"That's the only way I'll agree to do it."

He finishes his sandwich, downing his water after, and crinkles the bottle. "I'm sure we can figure out some kind of arrangement." He waggles his eyebrows.

"Like I'm a hooker?"

"No!" he says loudly. "I mean..." But he must think about it and see my point. "Okay, fine. Pay whatever you want."

"Glad you finally came to see things my way." I smile.

When we're done eating, we walk out to the sidewalk and find Adam and Jed putting up the awning.

"Oh, you guys didn't have to do that," I say.

"It's either that or you break an ankle," Adam says, looking at Cade behind me.

I'm shocked to find Jed helping.

"I guess since you're not going anywhere," Jed says, climbing down after he finishes, "you might as well be official."

We all stare at the awning that has the words The Story Shop scrawled across it. Cade's front is to my back. Although we're not touching, I'm very aware of his presence.

Zoe from The Grind comes out and claps. "It looks awesome," she shouts from across the street.

Chuck steps out of the butcher's, and for the first time, I see a grin on his face. "Welcome, neighbor."

A few Sunrise Bay people stop and say how excited they are about the shop opening too, and a seed of happiness sprouts inside. Maybe things in this town are finally coming together. I have my store, a place to stay, and soon I'll have a way to get around. And then there's Cade, although I'm not sure for how long I'll have him.

It's almost too easy and too simple, but I'll enjoy it for as long as I can.

"Jed?" A woman's voice invades my bubble. "Cade?"

All four of us turn, but it's Adam's hand on my shoulder that tells me this is something I should be concerned about.

"Reese?" Cade says. I've heard the name enough to know she used to date Cade, but I have no idea how long or how serious it was.

"Reese." Jed rolls his eyes at Adam, her name falling from his lips with a very different tone.

Cade wraps his arms around Reese, and she closes her eyes and inhales. I know the scent she's smelling right now, and it makes me want to yank him away from her and say that smell is mine. But he doesn't belong to me.

"When did you get back?" he asks, as though they keep up with one another.

"Yeah, Reese, what brings you back?" Jed asks, disdain clear in his voice.

Now I'm all kinds of confused. Why would Jed hate her?

She's a blonde, but her hair is on the short side and it's straight. She glances over Cade's shoulder then up at the awning.

"Oh, you must be the Presley I heard about who's opening the new bookstore?" She walks away from Cade, but I know I'm not imagining the way his eyes are glued to her as she walks toward me.

I put out my hand. "Hi. Yes, I'm Presley."

After she shakes my hand, she peeks in the window and smiles. "It's so cute."

"Thank you."

"Oh, I'm Reese," she says, but doesn't give me a moment to respond before turning to Adam. "Adam." She holds her arms out as if she's his dear aunt who hasn't seen him in ages. "I'm so sorry about Lucy. My mom told me."

Adam's eyes flare, looking at Jed and Cade over her shoulder.

Cade never glances in my direction. Not once. His gaze is steady on Reese.

"I'm fine," Adam says.

"Yeah, he's found a new love of Motown that's getting him through," Jed chimes in.

Adam steps back and Reese moves to Jed as though the three of them are her own brothers.

"Jed, comedian as always." She hugs him, but it's brief because Jed doesn't reciprocate and looks at Cade the entire time her arms are around him as though he's telling his brother to get this disgusting thing off of him.

Cade wouldn't notice though because he's yet to look at anyone besides Reese.

"What's the Motown about, Adam?" She stands in the circle with us all, as though she doesn't understand that she's struck everyone speechless.

"Presley." Adam motions to me.

"Oh, you're a Motown girl?" Reese shakes her head as if music is actually playing.

"No, I just suggested he listen to whatever music wouldn't remind him of Lucy," I admit.

Cade finally looks at me and our eyes lock, a small smile forming on his lips.

"Oh, that's cute. I mean, I doubt that helps you sleep at night after your wife left you, but it's cute." Her tone has turned condescending. If she thought of this family as her own, she could maybe be less crass in her delivery.

"It does help, actually." Adam eyes me.

I shrug. I don't really give a shit what Reese thinks. All that matters is what Adam says.

"Anyway, my mom sent me to the butcher. You know her." She looks at Cade.

He nods.

I guess that's not the reaction she wanted, so she puts her hands on Adam's arm then Cade's. "I know it's about that time of year, so if either of you needs anything, let me know."

She leaves Adam's side and rises on her tiptoes to place a soft, lingering kiss on Cade's cheek. Jed rolls his eyes. I think we might actually have something in common now.

"Bye, guys. Nice meeting you, Presley. Can't wait until the grand opening."

"You too." I wave and smile, not meaning it. Here I thought the manipulative bitches were only back home. Turns out there are some in Sunrise Bay too.

"What time of year is it?" I ask quietly. I'm fairly sure I'm overstepping, but I hate the fact Reese knows more than me.

"Our mom's birthday," Adam says.

"Hey." Jed clasps Cade's shoulder. "I need help for a second. Something's come up with a client..."

Jed doesn't fool me though. He's tearing Cade away to get a grip on himself before I grow suspicious. But Jed is underestimating me again. Cade and Reese have some sort of long history and what scares me is that he might think she's worth more than just a friends with benefits relationship like we have.

Chapter Twenty-one

"I heard the rumors."

~Chevelle Greene

Cade

Jed practically shoves me into Truth or Dare. "What the hell?" he yells, but I'm barely able to form a sentence.

Reese hasn't returned home in at least five years. Seeing her again stirs up all those emotions from when we were young.

"What?" I ask.

"Not that I'm condoning it, but if you want any hope of having anything with Presley, you pretty much screwed yourself just now."

Presley's name takes me out of my trance. "Pretty cool how she did that with Adam, huh?"

"The Motown thing? Yeah, but I still think he needs to get laid. Get under someone else to get over Lucy. He's dodging my set-up." Jed puts a beer in front of me. I never even saw him fill it.

"Not everyone solves things by screwing people." I sip the beer to calm myself. "She looked good."

"Same money-grubbing girl as ever." Jed's hated Reese since high school. And I can't say I don't understand why. "I'd take Presley over her any day."

"Since when did you join the Presley train?"

"Since Reese's train pulled into town. She's nothing but trouble."

I know she is and I'm not thinking of rekindling anything with her, but she was so much a part of my life, it's hard not to have all those feelings rush to the surface with her unexpected appearance. She was the only girl I was ever honest with about my mom dying and the responsibility I felt toward my family. Jesus, she's the only person other than my dad I've ever allowed to see me cry. All that doesn't disappear just because we broke up.

"What's going on with you and book girl?" Jed asks.

I sip my beer, not sure if I should tell him. I don't want it getting around. But then, Reese's appearance reminds me of how much I can trust him. He proved that long ago.

"We make out sometimes." I shrug as though it's no big deal.

He rolls his eyes. "You know it's only going to end with trouble, right?"

"What's that mean?"

"Don't get me wrong." He hops up to sit on the back counter. "It's great that she's brave enough to stick around, open a new store, and give it a go. The whole finding yourself thing is great, and so far, she looks awesome doing it."

I quirk an eyebrow and he waves me off. "Relax, I don't wanna fuck her. But what if it doesn't last? I mean, if anything is evident, it's that she's not from around here. What happens if the bookstore doesn't take off? Do you think she'll try again with another business? Can she even afford to? She ran away from home once... what's to say she won't run away again? You're a Sunrise Bay lifer, but is she?"

"She doesn't have to be." I finish my beer and walk around to wash my glass. "There are no strings."

He hops down from the counter. "You're a smart guy, always did better than me in school, and even I don't believe that."

Whether my brother believes it or not, it's true. Presley didn't expect me to spend the night last night. She lectured me about bringing her breakfast. She's getting her own car. There are no signs that she wants anything more than my dick.

"It's working for us," I say.

"One day you're gonna be knocked on your ass when this goes to shit." He disappears down the hall.

When someone knocks on the window, I turn toward the front. It's Presley. She gives me a small wave.

I head over and open the doors of the brewery. "Hey."

"Hi. I just wanted to thank Jed for putting up my awning and give you this." She hands me an envelope with the word *rent* in girly script on the front.

"I told you—"

She puts up her hand. "I feel the need to make the point even more pointed that I'm *just* a tenant."

"You don't have to pay to stay there."

"Oh, and I asked Zoe if she wouldn't mind giving me a ride to the car rental place tonight. It's on her way home, so that way I'm not disturbing you."

Jed comes walking out from out of the back.

"Hey, Jed, thanks again for helping Adam with the awning. I really appreciate it."

He waves. "No problem." He pretends he forgot something and goes back down the hall.

But she's already walking away. "See you later."

"Presley," I call after her.

She puts her hand in the air. "I've got a million things to do. A new shipment just came in. See ya."

I watch her open the door of her shop and disappear inside.

"Things already went to shit, didn't they?" Jed asks as if he never left. "Leave it to Reese to screw it up for you."

Just as he says her name, she walks out of the butcher, so I shut the door and lock it as if keeping her physically out of my brewery will stop her from invading my life once again.

CHEVELLE WALKS into the house and covers her eyes. "Fisher, ew. Put on some pants."

"We bathed together." He continues playing Xbox with Jed, not even glancing in her direction.

"As babies. This is very different," Chevelle says.

Jed laughs. "I don't mind seeing your junk, Fisher."

"I'm comin' off a long damn shift, Chevelle, so I suggest you get yourself a blindfold if you don't like it."

I pick up a piece of pizza and relax in the chair, enjoying not having any attention pointed my way. Plus, the chair gives me the perfect view of the driveway, so I'll know when Presley comes home. As it grows darker, I worry she doesn't know her way around.

"So, Mom's birthday," she says, plopping down on the couch next to Fisher. But she's perched on the end and turned in my direction.

A car pulls up the drive and I lean over to get a better

view out the window. It parks behind Fisher and I sigh when I see it's Fisher's best friend, Cameron's, Jeep. Damn it. Where the hell is she?

Cameron knocks and we all yell to come in. He steps into the room and Chevelle sighs.

"Hey, Cam, I'm almost done obliterating your friend." Jed tilts his whole body as if it controls what's happening on the screen, his fingers moving a mile a minute.

"Like hell." Fisher's body moves and comes dangerously close to touching Chevelle, who watches him as if he's a snake slithering her way and she's deciding when it's time to abort mission.

I stand, annoyed and needing a distraction. "Hey, Cam." I bump his fist. Cam's been around since we were young.

Chevelle gets up to move over to my chair, but Cam quickly sneaks in and she ends up on his lap. He's always treated her like a little sister too.

She smacks his shoulder, annoyed. "You're so annoying!"

"Feel free to stay, I don't mind you on my lap," Cam jokes—to antagonize her or Fisher, I'm not sure.

Fisher drops his controller and narrows his eyes at Cam while Jed screams in victory.

Jed stands and puts his hand in the air for a high five from Cam. "Thank you very much."

Fisher's still glaring at Cam, but Chevelle follows me into the kitchen.

She sits at the kitchen table and pulls out a piece of paper. "I have the itinerary."

This has been Chevelle's thing ever since our mom died. I know it's a part of her healing and the therapist said that if it helps her, then we should keep it up. But it's been years now and we're all grown up. I'd prefer we all just grieve her ourselves. Not that I'm going to bring up that idea.

"I figure I can get the flowers and we can meet there at the same time as always. We'll each say something to Mom like always and then we'll all go to Dad and Marla's to eat."

This whole day she's talking about is for Fisher, Xavier, Adam, Chevelle, and me. After Dad married Marla, we excused him because we didn't want her to feel bad. But he still comes every year and Marla is perfectly comfortable with it. She's an amazing stepmom.

"Sounds fine." I grab a beer out of the fridge. "Want a drink?"

"No, I'm good." She tucks her blonde hair behind her ears. "Do you need to talk?"

I sit at the table and look at her. "Why?"

"You seem antsy, and I mean, I heard the rumors."

I blow out a breath. "What rumors?" I act dumb, but I'm sure tomorrow Nikki will be talking all about it anyway.

"Reese being back. I heard her boyfriend cheated on her with her best friend, so she came home. Someone else said she's back for good." Her eyes widen.

"That sucks for her, but I don't really care." I tilt back my head and gulp down my beer.

"Okay then, do you want to talk about Presley?"

Chevelle was only five when our mom died, and she's struggled with that loss her entire life—for reasons that are her own and completely understandable given what happened. I've been there as much as I could to listen and help guide her, so it's no surprise that she wants to reciprocate with me, but that's not the way our relationship goes. She's not going to be my confidante. She's got enough to deal with besides my bullshit.

"No, I don't."

She leans in across the table and lowers her voice. "Is what Nikki said true?"

"What?"

"That you and Presley are together?"

I'm not about to explain to my twenty-three-year-old sister about the friends with benefits situation I find myself in. "No. She's staying above the garage and that's it."

Thankfully Cam walks in and opens the fridge.

"You just let him go into your fridge?" Chevelle asks me.

"Relax, little one." He pulls three beers out of the fridge and goes back into the other room.

She rolls her eyes. I'm not sure why Chevelle and Cam have never gotten along, but if I had to guess, I'd say it's because Cam was at our house a lot and they developed a sibling rivalry of sorts. But I wish Cam would've stayed in the kitchen longer so he could help get her off my back.

"I have a poem I want to read this year," she says.

"Okay."

Honestly, I grieve my mom my own way. A way I've never shared with any of my siblings. So whatever Chevelle wants to do, I'm fine with it. But she wants me to okay it because I'm the oldest.

"Don't you want to hear it?" she asks.

"I'll hear it that day."

She nods. I can tell she wants to read it to me now, but I've got too much on my mind to think about something that's still weeks away. It's like the minute the first of the month happens, everyone is remembering her. Which is great, but I need some fucking air right now.

As though she's my saving grace, headlights reflect off

the garage. I stand to go meet Presley, but Chevelle stands faster.

"Oh, I haven't officially met her yet. Is that her?" She beelines past me, out the back door, and ambushes Presley the minute she parks her small rental SUV.

This is one of those times when big families suck.

Chapter Twenty-two

Presley

I exit my rental SUV as a slender woman with long blonde hair shoots out of the main house.

"Presley," she says.

Please tell me she's not another ex of Cade's. The first one has thrown me into a spiral I *just* managed to talk myself out of. I had to remind myself that he and I aren't anything special. We're fuck buddies, if I want to classify us as anything, even though we've yet to actually have sex. Something I'm unsure will ever happen now with Reese's appearance.

I freeze when she throws herself at me, wrapping her arms around me and squeezing tightly.

"Hi," I say, lengthening the word and standing like a statue.

"Presley, this is my sister, Chevelle." Cade's voice comes out of the darkness until he appears as a shadowy persona on the porch.

I notice the beer in his hand. Seeing Reese has stressed him out. Not a good sign for me.

Chevelle finally removes herself like a blanket from me. "It's so nice to meet you."

I nod. "You too." I reach in and grab my grocery bags, along with the bags from the retail store where I bought some trash cans and bedding.

"I love that you're staying up in the apartment. I used to have sleepovers up there when I was little."

Another Greene admission of how the space above the garage was used. It makes me wonder what Cade's memories up there might be.

She follows me up the stairs, as does Cade, both loaded with bags from my car.

"I can get it all," I say.

"Nonsense. We're right here." She steps in and places the bags on the counter. "Oh, you cleaned it up nice."

I put away the groceries while Cade stands there, drinking his beer.

"I should go. I just had to stop by to talk to Cade." Chevelle's gaze finds his, and he manages a smile for his younger sister. They obviously share a bond. She hugs me again on my way back from the fridge to grab more items. "Welcome to Sunrise Bay."

"Thanks." I can't help but smile at her, despite my mood.

"And don't go into the main house. Fisher is in there in his boxers."

"Consider me warned."

She hugs Cade and he pats her back, his gaze on me the entire time. Then she's gone and the door shuts, leaving a deafening silence in her wake.

I continue to put away the items, unsure where we

stand after I gave him rent as though I was making the point that he was free to do what he wanted. If that means he wants to do Reese again, so be it. I'm fully aware of how ridiculously needy I was being. I might as well have given him an ultimatum right there.

He sets down the beer and comes up behind me when I struggle to get a box on a high shelf. His hand lands on my hip and he eases the box out of my hand, setting it up on the shelf.

"Thanks," I say.

He doesn't move and I don't turn around. My breath feels heavy in my lungs.

"I feel like I need to apologize," he says in a low voice.

I squeeze my eyes shut and shake my head. "You did nothing wrong."

He slides my hair over to one side and goose bumps chase after his finger, my body betraying me again. I feel his breath before his lips touch my shoulder.

"I would have done all this with you," he says.

"That's not part of the agreement."

I turn around to try to leave, but his hand winds through my hair at the back of my head. His lips fall to mine and I sink into his hold. His kisses are like a glass of wine after a long day. I'm thankful the counter is behind me because just like with wine, I want to sigh and collapse into a comfy chair with a good book. Okay, well, I actually want to sink into a comfy chair and spread my legs for him.

When his lips are on mine, there's no fight in me to remember what this is and keep him at arm's length.

He breaks the kiss and steps back. "You probably want to finish putting the groceries away."

I'm about to say nah, the ice cream can melt, but I'm fairly sure I'll be needing that ice cream in the coming weeks, based on the fact that I willingly agreed to a friends with benefits relationship with a man I don't see as just a friend. That realization came when I found myself jealous of his ex earlier today.

"I should."

He unpacks the bags and I put everything away, Cade helping me with the top shelves. After we're all done, I ask him if I can use their washing machine and dryer. Then we head inside the main house, sneaking into the basement before anyone sees us.

I load the comforter and sheets I bought and I'm about to go back to my apartment when Cade picks me up by the hips and plops me down on the washer. His hands slide up my thighs, nudging them apart so he can fit between them. Grabbing my ass, he slides me forward.

"Are you offering me a ride on the spin cycle?" I say, the first joke we've had since Reese's reappearance.

"I'm in charge of your spin cycles," he says before his lips are on mine again.

There's something domineering about this kiss, a claim of sorts that I haven't felt from him yet. There's no possible way he's not still navigating his feelings about Reese's return, but this kiss feels like a declaration. He deepens it and I cling to him as though I'm afraid he's going to leave me.

He pulls back and rests his forehead on mine. "I like what we have going."

And that's enough for me. I naively agreed to this, but I'm not going to ignite a set of flares to alarm him and make him think I've caught feelings. I'm a grown woman and able to handle this relationship for what it is—unattached sex. So I nod slowly without saying a word.

"Let's go to your apartment," he whispers and picks me up, lowering me until my feet touch the floor.

"Don't forget the condoms," I say, walking up the stairs.

"I love the fact you put an s on the end of that sentence."

I smile back at him and leave him in his house while I head back to my apartment.

I'm only inside for a few minutes before I hear some kind of commotion from inside the house. I look out the curtains to see what's going on and watch as all the guys rush out of the house and get into Jed's truck.

My phone dings as the headlights disappear down the driveway.

Cade: *Sorry, our younger brother broke his leg. Rain check?*

Me: *Of course. Go.*

Cade: *I'm never going to be inside you, am I?*

At least it's something he still wants.

Me: *I'm here all night.*

Cade: *I'll keep you posted.*

Me: *Just worry about your brother.*

Cade: *Thanks for understanding.*

I send him a smiley face and fall to the bed, sexually

frustrated and messed up in the head. I thought I was trying to keep things uncomplicated.

I MAKE MYSELF DINNER, and after I finish moving my comforter to the dryer, I head back upstairs. I'm not gonna lie, it's a little scary coming to the main house at night with the woods surrounding us. But I don't have much of a choice.

The boys left their Xbox on, along with all the lights, and left the doors unlocked. So I turn off the game, wrap up the pizza, and throw the box in the trash outside. I turn off the lights and lock the front door. I have to keep the back door unlocked so I can get back inside to remove my comforter from the dryer.

Once I'm in my apartment, I arrange my bathroom with my new toothbrush holder and trash can. I put out some knickknacks I bought, but once I'm done, I'm restless and unsure what to do with myself. So I open the small door that leads to the unfinished portion of the garage.

My phone rings and I assume it's Cade, so I rush over to the bedside table and answer. "Hey. Is everything okay?"

"Sweetie, we booked our flights for your grand opening. We cannot wait." It's my mom.

I sigh, sinking to the bed.

"Are you okay?" she asks.

"I'm fine."

"Once we're in town, we'll get you back into Glacier Point. Wyatt called your dad to say how sorry he is."

I had no idea my dad even knew Wyatt's family until after Dad told his friend at the club that his daughter was in Sunrise Bay. Long story short and Wyatt was offering us a discount and saying how he'd take care of me while I was in Alaska. He's a nice guy and thankfully doesn't give off the stuck-up society asshole vibe I'm used to dealing with in our circles. Especially since his circle is a lot wealthier than mine.

"That's okay. I'm going to stay here. I already paid rent."

There's a long silence.

"You can't stay there."

"I can." I flex my jaw while I wait for her to speak.

"Rent is so... I mean, it's so permanent."

"Yes, Mom, because I'm opening up a bookstore, I'm going to be here for the foreseeable future."

Another long silence ensues, and I get up from the bed, annoyed, and go to the door to the unfinished part, finding a light switch by the door. Crouching through it, I see the boxes that Cade must have put away when I came up here.

I pry one open and pull out a football trophy with Cade's name on it. And then another one and another one. There's a yearbook and a homecoming sash with his and Reese's names. I slide the silky material through my fingers then toss it aside.

"Well, we'll talk when I land. Your dad wants to see your business plans anyway."

"Listen, I hate to do this, but I need to go."

"We just got on the phone," she whines.

"I'll call tomorrow. Promise. Love you."

"Love—"

I click off the phone before she finishes because I'm too preoccupied with the picture I'm holding. It's of a much younger Cade and Reese nestled together at some bonfire. His arms are around her and she has her head turned toward him with that same look she had on the sidewalk —love.

I pick up the yearbook and flip through the pages, seeing the Greenes everywhere in it. Cade and Jed together in football uniforms. All the Greene boys—Cade, Jed, Fisher, Xavier—in football gear. I scan the pages, reading some messages his high school friends wrote to him. Then there's a long message that takes up an entire page and I don't bother reading it until I see who signed it. *Love you forever, Reese.*

No one would have the self-control not to read it, I'm sure. So I start at the top.

CADE,

I know we've had our problems this year, but you've been mine since we were freshmen. Probably earlier. We were voted most likely to be high school sweethearts who'd marry and raise our children in Sunrise Bay. That says something. Since we're going to different colleges, I wanted to let you know—after I'm done, I'm coming home to start my life with you. It's always been us. I hope by the time that happens, you've forgiven me for whatever you think I've done. I love you, Cade, all of my life. Nothing will change that.

Love you forever,
Reese

SHE'S WRITTEN the last e in her name as a heart. How cute.

I slam the book shut. I wonder if that's the reason she's back now, even if she's years behind schedule—to lay her claim on him.

A little voice inside my head says, are you going to claim

him? With all my issues I need to work through, I am not the person for Sunrise Bay's golden boy.

Stuffing everything back in the box, I close it up and head back to my own area. Now I feel worse. Serves me right for being a snoop.

I lock my door and walk down the steps into their house with 911 in my phone and my finger hovering over the green button. Down in the basement, I grab my comforter and sheets from the dryer, clean out the lint trap, and shut the dryer door. I tiptoe up the stairs, but then a large figure appears in the doorway and blocks my way.

I scream and fall backward, my phone slipping from my hands.

Chapter Twenty-three

Cade

"Shit," Fisher says and barrels down the basement steps.

I follow him to find Presley at the bottom of the steps, her comforter over her face.

"What the hell?" I run down the stairs, my heart in my throat.

"I was just curious why the door was open and the light was on." He squats to check on her.

"Presley?" I say, taking all the sheets off her to see if she's conscious.

"I'm fine. Just a sore ass," she says, but her hand is on her head.

Fisher puts all her stuff in her laundry basket, and I help her to her feet.

"Go slow," I say.

"My phone." She frantically looks around.

There's a glow coming from the bottom of the stairs and Fisher goes over and picks it up, clearing the screen. He tosses it in the laundry basket. "Good job having 911 on your phone, but next time, press the green button."

"I don't think you need to lecture her on safety right now," I tell him.

"It's a proven fact that you should do it now when she's still reeling from being scared."

"Oh really, where did you hear that?"

"When we were training the new K-9 unit," he sneers.

"She's not a dog," I grind out.

Presley puts both of her hands in the air. "Stop it, you two."

I help her up to the kitchen and sit her on a chair then grab a bag of peas from the freezer. Who knows how long this bag has been in there since it's only used for injuries. Putting it on the back of her head, she sighs, her eyes closing.

"She can't fall asleep for an hour at least. Maybe we should take her in," Fisher says.

"Not a bad idea." I move to pick her up. Better to be safe.

"I'm not going anywhere. I'm fine. Just give me a minute." She closes her eyes again,

Yeah, we're not going to play this way.

"We're going." I lift her. The fact that she's not trying to get out of my arms says she's not so sure herself.

"I'll go with you," Fisher says.

"No, you have a shift. I'll be fine. Marla and Dad are there anyway."

Rylan broke his leg at soccer, so he's at the hospital, waiting to get casted. To him, it feels like a life sentence since he can't play for a while. Jed and Adam dropped us off and went to the sports place to pick up Rylan's stuff.

"You gotta keep her awake, man," Fisher says.

"I'm good. Just help me get her in the truck."

But after her body slumps against me, I take Fisher up on his offer. With Fisher's help, I get Presley in the truck and take us to the hospital, Fisher telling her over and over again to keep her eyes open.

I drop the two of them off at the emergency room doors of our small hospital here in Sunrise Bay, park, and head inside. She's already in a room when I reach them, thanks to Fisher's connections.

Marla comes out of Rylan's room, looking confused. "He's fine, Cade."

"I know. I'm here for someone else."

She follows me to the room where we find Fisher is staring at Presley, a flashlight in her eyes. A nurse is getting her vitals.

"What happened?" Marla asks.

"Fisher scared the hell out of her, and she fell backward down the basement stairs."

"She's responding well, but we'll need to get a CT scan," the nurse says.

"Thanks, Allie," Fisher says.

I hold Presley's hand and use my free hand to smooth her hair, whispering to help keep her awake.

"I'm fairly sure she's here overnight." Allie squeezes Fisher's shoulder and leaves the room.

I stare at him until he notices and asks, "What?"

"How close of a relationship do you have with Nurse Allie?" I ask.

"None of your fucking business," he says.

"Fisher, language, and he's right, Cade, it's none of your business," Marla says.

"Since when?" I ask. "Apparently my life is a fucking open book."

"Language," Marla says. "I'm going to go tell your dad what's going on. I'll be back."

She leaves the room and I look at Fisher. "I'm staying with her. You can take my truck back to the house."

He stands as though he wants to leave, which surprises me since Nurse Allie is obviously perfecting her bedside manner with Fisher. "Call Clara."

I shake my head.

"Her sister can stay with her. I mean, are you two like..." He waits for me to fill in the blank, which I'm not going to do.

"I want to be here, jackass. Try it sometime. You might enjoy it."

He rolls his eyes and leaves the room.

A doctor comes in, and Presley groans as he tries to give her a neurological exam. But she gets through it. Allie was right—Presley is staying overnight.

"Does she have family we should call?" the doctor asks me.

"No, it's just me," I answer.

It's then I realize how different our lives are. She has her parents and Clara, but that's all I really know. I can't imagine not having a hospital room full of people—like Rylan just did for a broken leg.

Sure, I could call Clara or even Presley's mom, but her mom's in Connecticut. She wouldn't get here until the morning, if that. From what I gather, they have money and people with money do pull off some things fast, but she can't stop time. And I will call Clara—once I know exactly what's going on. For now, I'll be the one who's here for Presley.

It sinks in how strong she is for coming to this town all by herself, not having anyone who has her back.

"I'm going to put her in a gown. Maybe you want to step out," Allie says.

"I can do it."

"Um. You're not even related and—"

"He can do it," Presley mumbles. "He's seen me naked."

Allie smirks as I take the gown from her and close the curtain.

"This is not how I wanted to undress you tonight." I get Presley to sit up and I take off her shirt and her bra, wishing like hell we were in bed and I had a box of condoms on the nightstand.

"Me either. How is your brother?" she asks.

I kiss her temple and get the gown over the front of her, then I unbutton, unzip, and pull her jeans off of her. "He'll be fine until I kick his ass for scaring you."

I pull the blanket over her, fold up her clothes, and put them on the vacant chair.

"I meant your other brother."

"He's fine. It was a clean break. But don't be surprised if we get a visitor in here named Marla Greene, my stepmom."

She giggles and seems more alert now.

A man wearing scrubs walks in. "I'm going to take her for a CT scan."

I kiss her forehead and whisper that I'll be here when she returns.

I wish I could go with her. I'm not gonna lie, seeing her at the bottom of the basement stairs freaked me out. But I push all those thoughts from my mind because I am *not* falling for her. I'd have felt as if I'd been gut-punched regardless of who was lying at the bottom of the basement stairs. It means nothing.

I wait anxiously, the minutes passing like hours until she's wheeled back into the room. The doctor says she's okay to fall asleep since her eyes aren't dilated and she hasn't thrown up, but until they get the results of her test and make sure it doesn't show any signs of a serious concussion I'll still worry.

I snuggle on the chair with the blanket they give me and wrap her hand in mine until I fall asleep, ignoring the fact that it comes easy because she's near.

"AREN'T THEY THE CUTEST?" Marla coos, her voice waking me.

It takes a moment for me to figure out where I am—until I glance next to me and see Presley all snuggled in the fetal position. Our hands are intertwined. I slide my hand out from hers.

"Marla. Dad. Hey, Rylan."

He stands with his leg in a cast, the crutches holding his weight.

"We're just on our way home," Marla whispers. "How are things here?"

She comes up beside the bed and I figure she won't be leaving anytime soon. She's like a younger Grandma Ethel.

"Good. The test came back and said she has a mild concussion, so they're just observing her."

"That's good."

Presley stirs, and when her eyes flutter open, she jolts back. I chuckle. You can tell she doesn't come from a big family.

"Hey, Presley, heard you took a bit of a tumble," my dad says.

"Yeah." Her cheeks pinken a bit.

"Hi, Presley, I'm Marla." Marla speaks to her as if Presley's hard of hearing.

"Mom," Rylan says as though he's annoyed with her.

I've been there. Dad squeezes Rylan's shoulder just like he used to do with me, to caution me in a polite way not to make a scene. Rylan says nothing more, so obviously the method is still effective.

"Hi, Marla." Presley slides up on the bed, her hands going to her hair and running under her eyes. Her makeup is smeared and her hair is a little matted, but she's still the most beautiful woman in here.

"So I know this is crazy, but I've been meaning to come by. We'd love to have you over for dinner."

I clear my throat and I'm granted my dad's death stare.

Presley looks to me as though she needs my approval, so I say, "You should go. Have fun, and I'll catch you when you're done."

Marla laughs and her gaze fixates on Presley. "He's just kidding. So how about this Thursday? We'll do it before the town meeting, then everyone can walk over."

"Oh. Okay. Where do you live?"

"Cade will bring you." Marla looks at me.

I nod. "I'll take you. It's near the downtown area."

Presley nods. "Okay."

"Great. Then we'll see you then."

Presley opens her mouth, but no sound comes. She swallows. "What can I bring?"

"Just yourself." Marla waves and touches Presley's leg. "Hope you get out soon."

"Feel better, Rylan," I say, watching them all go.

Dad didn't say one word, although I could feel his presence as usual.

Only in the Greene family are you not in charge of

setting up the meet-the-parents. Then again, Presley isn't going to my parents' house as my girlfriend and she already knows my dad. She's going on Marla's invitation because Marla wants to meet the new girl in town.

"Are you sure you want to go?" I ask.

"You can go. You don't have to stay with me," she says, changing the subject.

"I don't know, I was thinking..." I look around. "Maybe we test out these hospital beds."

I slide up into the bed with her. After a lot of thinking after the doctor came in and she was still sleeping, I'm pretty sure she's not used to people being there for her. I'm going to be her person. I mean, isn't that included in the friend's portion of friends with benefits? To sleep next to her while she recovers from a concussion my brother caused? I'm sure Xavier would agree.

Chapter Twenty-four

"She's not the threat."
-Marla Greene

Presley

Thursday comes fast, and I'm not prepared to have dinner at the Greene's. My stomach has been stirring all day.

Cade took the doctor's orders seriously when he said no strenuous activity for a week, so other than a few hot make-out sessions and Cade devouring my breasts, we still haven't had sex. I'm starting to think the benefits portion of our agreement will never involve sex. But so far, I haven't had to see Reese again and I kind of like it that way.

At the end of the workday, Cade walks through the back door of my shop. Since Adam is finished working here and my grand opening hasn't happened yet, it's a little lonely.

"Not you too," he says in my ear from behind me because "You Can't Hurry Love" by The Supremes plays from my Bluetooth speaker.

"I kind of like it." My hands cover his, and he kisses my neck.

"Ready then?" he asks, stepping back.

"I'm going to wear my overalls just to tempt you to cross the line." I lift the hem of my shirt in a seductive dance.

"We've got three more days," he says, tapping his nonexistent watch.

"Then it's on. You better clear time on your calendar, because I don't expect to leave my bed all day. You're going to need the wholesale box of condoms."

"Yes, ma'am." He chuckles.

"I'm just saying, so far the benefits are weak."

"Are you suggesting my Kielbasa isn't filling you up?"

"I want it to fill another part of me." I turn on the lights by the window to light up the showcases I just set up and lower the lights on the interior of the store.

Cade stops me before I can go through the back door, his hands running up my outer thighs and around until he reaches the apex of my thighs. "Have I told you I love the warmer weather? I love you wearing skirts and how easy it is to tease you." His finger runs along my clit over my panties. I grow wet with his touch.

I slap his hand. "Three days, remember?"

"Now we're on the same page."

I grab my purse and jacket because spring in Alaska is still chilly at night. Once I'm ready to go, we walk out the back door and I lock up. He reaches for my hand but retracts it—remembering we're in public, I suppose. Although I'm wondering who wouldn't know we're fooling around at this point.

We round the downtown parking lot, leaving his truck in the back since we're walking to his parents' house. He stops me right before we're about to be in front of everyone, backs me to the brick wall of the shop, and looks around. Then his lips are on mine and his tongue is in my mouth.

The kiss happens so fast, I'm a fumbling mess when he stops and we both inhale a deep breath.

"Sorry, I had to do that before I lost my chance," he says.

He waits for me to walk the streets of downtown Sunrise Bay. Most of the stores are closing for the day, but from what I hear, tourist hours are starting in ten days with my grand opening. I guess it's a big thing here.

"Who doesn't know about us?" I ask. Clara came by the other day with twenty questions and I didn't cave, but I'm fairly sure all his brothers know.

"I think people probably assume, so it's all about whether we want to confirm the rumors or not, I guess."

"So we walk around like we've become best friends?"

"Unless you want them to know." He shrugs.

"No." I clear my throat. "I mean, we shouldn't, right? Since it's not a *real* relationship."

He stops us when we reach the end of the square and we're about to cross the street toward a huge house on the hill. Is that his family's house? I thought it was a museum above the start of the town. He tugs me into a small alley. I never knew there were so many hiding spots around here. I kind of like it.

"It doesn't matter what we tell people. They're going to believe what they want. There are people in this town probably rooting for you to break my heart or vice versa. Others swear we're soul mates. Others are indifferent. Others are optimistic but doubtful because of our pasts."

"And you?"

He hovers over me, his arm pressed against the wall. "I like you a lot. And I'm enjoying the friendship we've developed along with all the fooling around, but I'm assuming all the reasons that made us decide to be friends with benefits still stand? They haven't changed. But if this is getting too close for comfort, we can call it off."

Talk about your heart falling to the pit of your stomach. He just released a wrecking ball on me. Not that I didn't already know it, but hearing him confirm that nothing has changed for him in these past weeks is hard to swallow. I guess small-town manners and expectations are why he took me to the hospital, gave me a place to stay for minimal rent, and is making sure this week isn't too strenuous for me.

"No." I shake my head, lying through my teeth. "I'm great with how it is. We're on the same page."

I guess maybe it's not a complete lie. All the reasons I shouldn't be in a relationship right now are still there. They still hold weight. Hell, he just proved them correct. I'm already suffering from the fear of abandonment, which is why his words cut so deep. I had to go and find the one unavailable sweet guy in Sunrise Bay. It's like a running joke on me. Happily ever after for Presley Knight. Then an evil laugh cuts in... NEVER!

"We should go. I don't want to be late," I say, wanting desperately to leave this conversation behind.

"You sure we're okay?" There's genuine concern in his eyes.

Cade isn't a bad guy. He didn't change the rules—I did.

"I'm great. Just wanna make sure we can make it to the dinner and meeting."

He gives me a chaste kiss. No tongue thankfully. I'm pretty sure I wouldn't have the gusto to give him a kiss that wouldn't make him second-guess my lie that I'm fine.

We walk up the hill toward the big house that is in fact his parents'. He doesn't ring the doorbell but walks right in, and I hear a lot of voices in what I assume is the kitchen at the back of the house. He takes off my coat and purse and puts them in a room near the entryway.

He lets me walk in first, but I stop upon entering and he runs right into my back.

"Reese stopped in just to say hello," Mr. Greene says as Marla slams the fridge door closed, turning around with a bottle of white wine in her hands.

This is the fucking cherry on top of the damn sundae of disappointment.

WE ALL END UP sitting in the formal dining room, Reese across from Cade, Rylan across from me. Thankfully, no other siblings are here tonight to witness my mounting humiliation and frustration, though it makes it more awkward that it's just the six of us.

"My mom wanted to make sure I dropped off her famous brownies to Mr. Greene. She always did have a thing for you," Reese coos.

Marla brings her wine glass to her lips, clearly a fake smile on her face even though I barely know the woman.

"Until Marla snuck into town and snatched your heart away," Reese adds.

I drop my napkin and it falls to the floor.

"Let me," Cade says from beside me.

"No, I've got it." I have to pick it up because I'm paranoid her foot is in Cade's crotch.

It's not, so I pick up my napkin and place it on my lap, then cut up the chicken Marla made. She's a great cook. Either that or my taste buds are having a party over the first home-cooked meal I haven't made for myself in forever. Her salad dressing is awesome, and when I remark about it,

Reese helpfully informs me that Marla bottles it and sells it nearby.

Marla looks annoyed that Reese is the one to speak up about her business, so I direct my next question directly to Marla. "How come you never made this bigger?"

"Once Rylan was born, I just didn't have the energy. I'm happy with what I sell locally."

"It's really good."

"Remember that time I was here, and you had all the kids try out your new flavors?" Reese adds.

"Yes," Marla says. "If I recall, you weren't fond of any of them."

"I was picky when I was a teenager. Oh my God, Cade, remember how we went to homecoming senior year and you took me to that nice restaurant and I only had a salad?"

"And I had to pay for an entire meal you didn't eat. Yeah." I can't tell from Cade's voice whether he's annoyed by the memory or not.

She looks at me. "It was supposed to be some sort of chicken, but it looked raw and had this gross sauce."

I nod and chew my salad. "How's the leg, Rylan?" I ask to stop Reese from traveling any farther down memory lane.

"It's good."

"I saw you had some signatures on it. Can I sign when we're done eating?"

He nods, eating his chicken. "Yeah. I went to watch one of my team's games and a bunch of people signed my cast."

"Calista Bailey was one of them." Mr. Greene's gaze works its way from Marla to Cade in a suggestive way.

"Stop it, Dad. We only train together," Rylan says, but his cheeks fill with a nice shade of pink.

"Oh, Rylan, maybe you and Calista will end up being like Cade and I were. You never know. We started off as friends in elementary school, too." Reese's soft eyes land on Cade's.

I don't have the energy to look at Cade, so I sip my wine like Marla and concentrate on Rylan. "What's Calista like? As a teammate, I mean?"

He shrugs. "She's good. It's her uncle who's training us."

"He was a well-known soccer player. Played in the MLS," Mr. Greene adds.

"Oh, that's awesome. I bet he knows his stuff then?" I look to Rylan for confirmation.

"Yeah, and he pits us against one another. She's good. Like real good."

"So are you," Cade says. "When you control your temper."

Rylan nods as though he knows this lecture by heart.

"Don't let him fool you. Your brother had a temper when it came to football," Reese says.

"Christ," I say and everyone at the table freezes. One quick glimpse at Marla and her wide smile confirms I did just say that out loud. *Shit.* "Sorry, I just remembered something. I need to call my mom." I stand from the table and place my napkin on the chair. "I'll be right back."

I hide in the bathroom, trying to compose myself. A soft knock lands on the door and I'm expecting it to be Cade, asking me what the problem is. But Marla's head peeks in after I say to come in.

She shuts the door behind her, squatting down along the wall next to me, and places her hand on my knee. "She's not a threat, if that's what you're thinking."

"What? Oh no, I just hung up with my mom. It's her birthday. I forgot."

But her eyes scour my lap and the area around me, not seeing a phone anywhere. She's got me.

"Well, if you were worried for some reason, don't be. She's not the threat."

I clue into her words. "But you're suggesting there is one."

She inhales deeply and looks toward the door then back at me. "Yes. I can see he likes you, but there's a giant wall you'll have to break down in order to get him."

"I don't understand. There isn't another girl?"

She smiles and shrugs. "Kind of, but not who you think. I have a great feeling about you two and I think you're the girl who's finally going to get to him, but only time will tell. I just don't want you to be jealous of Reese. She might want him, but Cade doesn't want her."

She leaves the bathroom before I can ask for more clarification. Thanks for dinner and the cryptic message, Marla.

I walk out of the bathroom to find Cade following Reese out the back door. I think Marla needs to check her notes again.

Chapter Twenty-five

"Beer and Books."
- Jed Greene

Cade

When did my life become so complicated?

Presley is clearly worried about Reese while Reese is dead-set on making Presley feel like an outsider. The conversation Presley and I had in the alley probably wasn't the best one to have right before we came to my dad and Marla's for dinner, but I didn't want to play her. I wanted to be honest.

"Can I talk to you?" Reese asks.

I glance at my dad and he pretends to be eating, never one to get into my business. I'm not gonna lie, we both thought Reese was the one for me at one point in our lives. But that feeling ended well before I ever left for college.

I wipe my mouth with my napkin and stand, leaving it beside my plate. "Sure."

She walks to the back door and I follow her onto the patio of what was my grandmother's house. My grandpa built this house, but my dad put a lot of work into it. The pergola over the porch with lights strung overhead allows us to see one another. The pool is closed up, and since all the outside furniture is still packed away, we have no choice but to stand.

"Is it serious?" she asks.

I stuff my hands in my pockets. "I'm not sure that's any of your business."

She turns around slowly. "So if I kissed you right now, what would your reaction be?"

"I'd push you off me, but that's not because of Presley."

Her shoulders sag. "It's been how many years? How are you not over it?" Her raised voice makes me think she still believes she did nothing wrong.

"I am over it, but that doesn't change the trust issue."

She throws her hands in the air. "Trust? I've always been your confidante. Remember I'm the one—"

"Enough with the 'remember when' shit. It's been twelve years since senior year and the only reason you want me now is because your boyfriend cheated on you."

She balks. "What? Who told you that?"

I say nothing because she's a Sunrise Bay lifer. She knows how the gossip spreads.

"It might be the reason I'm back, but it's not the reason I'm here with you now. It's always been us, Cade. Our story—"

"Our story died when you threw yourself at Jed."

"He's a liar."

During senior year, I broke up with Reese because she was just as intrigued as our classmates about Jed when he arrived in town. After he stole my quarterback position, she cozied up to him. Everyone thought I was being rash in my decision to break up with her. Months later, I thought maybe I had too, but after I got the quarterback position again, she was back at my side. Months later, after Jed and

I had become friends and football season was over, he came to me one night and confessed that Reese had approached him earlier in the season. He'd turned her down because she was my girlfriend, but she didn't let it go until coincidentally, I became the first-string quarterback again.

"He's my brother."

"Step."

I shake my head. "He's my brother."

"Just like you said, that was ages ago. We can start over. Whatever you have with her—"

"Presley," I say.

"It's temporary. She's not from around here. She doesn't know how things work and I doubt she's sticking around. It's easy with me. I know your past already, you don't have to open yourself up to someone new." She steps forward. "You can just be you and not trudge through all those feelings about your mom. I understand the hurt you went through, because I was here."

I take her hands before they touch me and lower them. "No, Reese. Whether or not I'm with Presley in the months ahead doesn't factor in on the fact that there will never be an *us* again."

She huffs and drops her arms to her sides. "You have no idea what you're missing out on. There was a reason we were happy. You're forgetting all of that because of one stupid thing."

Convenient how she admits it now, even though I knew all along that Jed was telling the truth.

The back door opens, and Presley slides out. "Hey, I'm going to get to the meeting now. I'll meet you over there." She's got her coat and purse on.

"No." I step toward her. "I'm coming with you."

I grab her hand, leading her into the house, and hear Reese's sigh behind us.

We say our goodbyes as my dad puts on his coat. "You sure you don't want a ride? Rylan's coming and he's not that good on his crutches yet."

I look at Presley. "I'm good."

Reese comes in the back door and helps Marla clear the table.

"I've got it, Reese, but thank you." Marla waves to us. "I'll see you all over there."

We walk out before Reese leaves, and as soon as we're outside, Presley whips her hand out of mine.

"What's that for?" I ask.

"Don't use me as some sort of toy," she says.

"What are you talking about?"

"If you want her, have her. If you don't, then fine. But holding my hand in front of her, when you made it pretty clear before we got here that was a hard pass?"

Maybe that wasn't my brightest moment.

She walks down the driveway toward downtown. When she reaches the area where we had the conversation on the way to dinner, she circles to face me. "Listen, I'm in this whole friends with benefits situation, but you will not embarrass me publicly." She pokes me in the chest. "I'm not some plaything. You want this kept a secret? Fine. Then no hand-holding, even when you want to make an ex-girlfriend jealous."

She's right. I'm an idiot. Although I was just trying to get Reese to back off, rather than make her jealous. But Presley's right, I can't use her as a pawn.

I cage her to the brick wall, move one hand to her hip, and my other cradles her face as my lips land on hers with a kiss I hope conveys how sorry I am. Like every time we touch, her body melts into mine and a slow moan leaks from deep in her throat. I've slowly become addicted, and part of me is scared for the first time we have sex. What if, for some reason, it's not as great as everything we've experienced up until now?

A group walks by and I step back, although they can't possibly see us in the dark of the alley.

"I'm sorry. It won't happen again," I say. "But I will say, I wasn't trying to make her jealous, just see that the two of us wouldn't ever be together again."

She nods. "Thank you for apologizing. Now let's go." She walks out of the alley.

"That's it?"

She looks over her shoulder. "Well, yeah."

Damn, that was easier than I figured it'd be.

MY DAD, Rylan, and Marla are all here before we arrive. Since Jed is in town, I opt to sit in the audience with Presley while he takes our seat on the panel. According to the flyer, we're discussing the next duo night, Presley's grand opening, and the beginning of tourist season.

George bangs the gavel. Clara runs up the aisle and sits next to Presley, Xavier right behind her. It's nice having him home during the off-season.

"The committee has met privately to discuss the issues and we've decided to try something new," George says.

Presley looks at me and my forehead crinkles. Jed dodges eye contact with me, as does my dad. Not the best sign.

"Since the grand opening of The Story Shop is happening on the first day of tourism season, we've decided to hold the duo for the town the night before. And then we'll continue the duo the day of the grand opening. As always, tourism brings in more money to the duo nights, but since this is Miss Knight's first one, we'd like to do a soft duo night the night before."

"Who is she partnered with?" someone asks.

This is an amazing opportunity for any business. The town will advertise, and where masses congregate, people feel as though that's the place to be. I have no doubt this plan was put into place to make sure The Story Shop has the strongest opening it can.

My hand slides to touch Presley's knee, but I catch Clara watching, so I retract it, remembering we're in public. I just wish I could convey how happy I am for her because this is huge.

George bangs his gavel because he loves that damn thing. "We're sticking to what the town voted, so it's Truth or Dare Brewery and The Story Shop."

"Beer and Books," Jed yells and winks. We'll have a talk later that he did this all behind my back.

"Or Books and Beer," Presley says.

Jed shakes his head, but his grin says he appreciates her retort.

Clara grabs Presley's knee and wiggles it. "This is so awesome for you."

I've never been jealous like I am right now that Clara got to touch her and congratulate her first. Goddamn, what the hell is wrong with me?

"I feel a little overwhelmed right now." Presley fans her face and turns to me. "How on Earth do we morph books and beer?"

I shrug because I don't really know, but I'll help her figure it out. "I'm sure Jed's got ideas."

The four of us laugh.

"Then as long as Miss Knight is okay with the plan, it's a go." George hovers his gavel above the wooden plaque.

"Yeah, I'm good with it," Presley says and the room claps.

George bangs the gavel. "Now on to the next thing on the agenda."

They discuss the beginning of tourism season and what needs to be done. Mandi and a few other inns discuss their booking rates and reservations at restaurants. Chevelle says how many boat tours have been reserved, and Fisher discusses the extra patrolman we hired for the crowds.

Presley pulls out her phone and opens her notes app, typing things she wants to get done before opening day.

After the meeting is dismissed, Clara hugs Presley, and I catch a few people watching. It's their slightly opened mouths as they smile, watching the two sisters embrace, that reminds me why I'd never live anywhere else. People in small towns have one another's backs and want everyone to be happy.

"What do you need me to do?" Clara asks.

"Just get me your recommendation list for the young adult section. And could you be there for duo night? I know nothing of what it's going to entail, and if I'm pulled away, maybe you could give some people some book recommendations."

Clara nods. "Absolutely."

Jed walks over to me. "How mad are you?"

"We're a partnership for a reason."

He nods a few times. "I know. I know. You're just too close to the situation and I didn't know if you'd have concerns. This is good for us. Especially since we're going to announce the new flavor for the summer."

Jed's right. He's a great marketer and I don't blame him. I might've thought this was too much for Presley too soon and tried to stop it. But she's strong and determined. I watch as a few people congratulate her and say if she needs any help to just reach out.

Jed looks on like I am. "She's really become a member of Sunrise Bay, huh?"

"Seems so."

"Seems that for the first time in my life, I was wrong. I guess she does fit in a small town." He elbows me.

All I can do is nod because I can't take my eyes off of her. Happiness looks beautiful on her.

Chapter Twenty-six

"I just decided to clear my head for a second."
-Cade Greene

Presley

"I have no idea what to do," I admit, sitting at a table with Jed and Cade.

"Good thing for the two of you, you have me." Jed stands and grabs five bottles of beer that he sets on the table.

I pick up a quesadilla that Cade made for lunch. They're pretty damn good. It's their signature item, according to him and Jed.

"You need to pick out books that fit these tastes or titles," Jed says, sliding the beer bottles toward me.

I set down the quesadilla and pick up the bottles, examining the labels. "Razzle Dazzle, Naked Digger, Limp Donkey, No Stout For You, and Melting Heart."

"Razzle Dazzle is new for the summer, and Melting Heart was our Valentine one." Jed points at each. "So I thought you could use Razzle Dazzle for a summer read, Melting Heart for a romance book. For the other ones, I figure you can taste them and pair them as you think. I'm not much of a reader." He shrugs.

I chuckle and take a sip of Naked Digger before coughing. Though I'm not a beer person, it's growing on me. "Okay, leave these with me tonight. This is a great idea."

"We can give out samples and package six-packs and the book for people to buy together," Cade adds. "I'm thinking since you'll have a lot of traffic at the store from browsers, we can keep most of it over here, but we'll put up signs around your place advertising the sets."

Excitement builds inside me. "This is amazing. I love all the ideas."

"Great! As soon as you get me the books, I'll get with our marketing people and make up the posters. Send me over your logo." Jed heads into the back. I think this is making his year.

"He's happy," I say.

Cade hooks the toe of his boot under my chair and slides me closer to him. "Guess what?"

"What?" I sip the stout beer, which is definitely not for me.

"Only two days before you're cleared for action."

"It'd be five minutes if you'd loosen up the reins. I'm clearly fine."

His hands slides up the hem of my shirt, running along my bare back, as he kisses me. He's been big into making out and heavy petting. Last night we said we'd watch a movie and somehow our lips wouldn't separate. When he went back to his house, I felt a longing I knew wasn't good. My feelings for Cade are growing and soon heartbreak will be a consequence. I'll have no one but myself to blame.

I break the kiss because I have to get back to the store if I want to have all the displays up and ready, but I need to talk to him about my parents' imminent arrival. "So, my mom is coming for the grand opening. Both my parents are.

She knows nothing about us, so no worries, but she's nosy and pushy and..."

He kisses me again, this time without tongue. "It's fine. Let's remember you've been stuck with my family for a while."

I nod because he's right. Although I never think of it as being stuck. I enjoy his family a lot. "It's just a warning. If she catches a whiff of something between us, it might not be good."

"I can handle myself. I'm a big boy."

My hand slides between his legs. "You're definitely a big boy."

He slides closer as though we're not in front of the windows of the brewery and Jed isn't just down the hall in the office.

Damn, he's so sexy and gorgeous and sweet. The total package.

"I should go." I unwind myself from him and grab the stuff we were working on, including the five open beers.

"Okay. Want some help?" he asks, standing.

"Nope. I've got it. See you later."

I walk out of the brewery and into my shop before I exhale a deep breath. *Fix this, Presley.* I cannot keep pretending that my feelings don't exist.

But I don't want to be unhappy during my grand opening. This is supposed to be a fresh start where I'm on cloud nine, so I might as well live it up until then. After the grand opening and duo night, I'll break my own heart and be honest with him. I promise.

IT'S FINALLY the day we can have sex and I've been waiting for Cade all morning. Hell, I thought he'd be here at midnight, banging down my door with a bow on his dick. But it's now ten o'clock in the morning and nothing.

I open the curtain for the millionth time. His truck is in the driveway still, so he hasn't gone to work. I planned to work from home today and not go into the store since I figured I'd be on my back or straddling Cade most of the day. He must have told Jed he wasn't going in too—so why isn't he over here?

As I'm about to close the curtain, I see him come out of the house and walk toward his truck. Maybe he forgot to buy condoms and has to run to the store? He stops and I shut the curtain quickly, dodging away from the glass. Through a sliver of an opening, I see him look up at the apartment, but he doesn't make any move to turn this way. He walks past his truck toward a path in the forest I've noticed but never dared to go through.

Maybe he's waiting on me? Making sure I'm still cool with this? He has been a gentleman our entire time together. So I grab my sweatshirt, slide on my boots, and walk out of the apartment to follow him.

Every other truck is out of the driveway, so no one else is home. I follow the opening in the trees that Cade went through, careful not to step on too many branches. This path definitely hasn't been used in some time or only by a limited number of people. I push away branches as I walk, but I still don't see Cade and wonder if he ventured off the path.

I should probably go back to my apartment and wait, but that's not me. So I venture on, and soon I do spot Cade at the edge of a lake, squatting and staring out over the water.

For a moment, I soak in the vision of him in the middle of this pristine piece of nature. Like so many other times, I'm struck by how beautiful of a man he is—both inside and out. He must be deep in thought to not have heard me approach, so I turn to head back, feeling now that I might be overstepping. Whatever this lake means to him, he obviously doesn't want me involved.

I take a step back and a branch cracks loudly under my foot. Cade turns to face me, no expression on his face. He returns his full attention to the lake and I decide to take that as an invitation that he's okay having me here. Maybe he wants to open up. I know his mom's birthday is coming up and it's a big deal for the family. Maybe we're going to bridge that gap from friends with benefits to something more.

I wrap my arms around his stomach, pressing my cheek to his back. He stiffens for a second, but then relaxes and rests his hands over mine.

"Are you okay?" I whisper.

"Yeah, I was about to come up," he says. "I just decided to clear my head for a second."

He swivels in my hold, and his knuckles run down my face as his gaze fixes to mine. I ruined whatever this moment was for him.

"I can wait back at the apartment."

He shakes his head. "Don't be silly. We've been waiting for this moment for too long to waste any more time."

He puts his arm around my shoulders, and we walk away from the lake. I wish he'd trust me enough to tell me what's bothering him. Instead of barraging him with questions, I let us pretend we're like two teenagers who've waited for their parents to be gone for the night so we can have sex. Maybe that's what he needs right now. He takes my hand and leads me into my apartment, locking the door behind us.

"I can't wait to have you," he says before he kisses me and urges me to step backward toward the bed.

I thought this moment would be different. That I'd be hoisted up on some surface and my clothes would be torn off, but Cade surprises me by kissing me so slow and seductive that I'm unsure of exactly *what* is about to happen. His fingers float up my ribcage and wind around me, but he doesn't unclasp my bra. Instead, he pulls me closer to him. His warm hands run a searing path up and down my back as his tongue glides with mine.

I wind my arms around his neck and fist his hair. He's a great kisser and this sensual, slow thing he's got going on right now is driving me insane with want.

He backs me up and I feel the mattress behind my legs. The kiss comes to an end and he moves just enough of his weight forward for me to fall back onto the mattress. I stare at him, his eyes filled with a smolder that stirs a hunger inside me. This is a very different Cade than I've been with before.

He pulls off his shirt, and our gazes meet until he crawls up the bed and I scoot back. Soon the delicious weight of his body is on me, and I close my eyes, taking in the heat and hardness of him. One of his thighs slides between mine and he grinds his hard length into my hip.

Our mouths search out one another's again and he wraps a hand around my neck as he nips and sucks my bottom lip. His lips travel down my jawline to my throat.

"God, you're beautiful," he whispers, his hands sliding under my shirt and lifting it while his lips caress my body, stirring awake all my nerves.

My fingers thread through his hair, unable to not touch

him in some way. He slides down my body, situating himself between my thighs, and this time when he reaches back, he unlatches my bra.

With my help, we take off my shirt and bra, and he wastes no time in palming my breast while his lips clamp on to mine again. Our bodies slide together, unable to get close enough. All I want is to be naked and have our silky warm skin coast along the other's. But that doesn't seem to be in Cade's playbook. Although I crave the release I know is coming, this is a welcome change.

He rests his weight on his elbows and looks down at me. "How did we get so lucky?"

I blink and my finger runs down his abs, hooking in the waistband of his jeans. "We don't know how lucky we are just yet."

He smiles, but even I know that's not what he meant. I wonder if it's pre-sex talk. An obligatory statement to suggest we found the perfect friends with benefits situation. So I put my hand around his neck and tug him toward me, answering with a kiss.

Rolling him onto his back, I kiss his collarbone, making my way down his chest. He scoots up on the bed and watches me with one arm resting on the headboard, his other hand running circles on my arm, looking sexy as fuck. I unbutton his pants, and I can't help but glance at his magnetic eyes watching me with hunger. Sliding his pants down, I take his boxers too, leaving him naked on my bed.

"Your turn," he says. I shimmy out of my jeans, and right when my fingers dive into the sides of my panties, he holds up his finger and crawls toward me. "Allow me."

I'm not sure why I have shivers in the wake of his touch as my silk panties slide down my legs. Cade's seen me naked and has taken off my panties plenty of times.

He presses his lips right at the top of my pussy. "One of my favorite Presley things. But I have other plans today." His arm swings around my waist and he pulls me down on the mattress.

Resting on top of me, he nudges my thighs open with his knee. This is it. We're finally going to have sex after weeks of missed opportunities.

"Cade," I say, causing him to stop placing open-mouthed kisses up my neck.

He rests his weight on his palms and looks down at me. I say nothing because I'm not sure what to say now that he's looking at me. This moment feels bigger than we are.

He moves his thumb across my bottom lip. "I'll be right back."

But this mood is too perfect, and I don't want whatever this bubble we've found ourselves in today to pop, so I lock my legs around him. He looks at me, obviously puzzled.

"I have an IUD and I'm clean."

He pauses as though he's weighing the risks and rewards.

"Please. I want to feel you," I say.

"I'm clean." He nods and eases back into position.

The tip of him pierces my opening and his mouth falls back down to mine. Slowly, he pushes inside me, and I open myself to take all of him. When he's fully seated, he breaks our kiss to look at me. My fingernails dig into his shoulder blades and he slowly thrusts in and out of me.

I lose all thoughts, lost in the moment of us together. Tender kisses, gentle caresses, pants, and moans in the haze of the late morning. His touch is featherlight. A slow tremble begins deep inside me, but I clench it back, not wanting to come yet. Not wanting this moment to end.

He grunts from me clenching and his thrusts grow

faster, more commanding. My body responds to everything he's giving me. I feel as though I can't get him close enough, so I bring his head down and smash my lips to his while my fingers claw at his skin, desperate to have him pull that pleasure from me.

His demands from my body become too much for me to stave off my climax any longer, and I clench around him as my orgasm consumes me. My back arches off the bed and I cry his name. When I open my eyes again, Cade is staring at me in what I can only think is wonder. He pumps into me three times before he stills, his stomach jolting from the force of his own orgasm.

He falls on me, not pulling out right away, and we both lie in my bed, our hands wandering over each other with touches of tranquility.

Holy shit, I think we just made love. That's definitely not something friends with benefits do, but I'm going to enjoy this moment a little longer before I deal with reality.

Chapter Twenty-seven

"Let her be tonight."
-Adam Greene

Cade

The minute I pull out of Presley, I still.

Her fingers thread through my hair with a sensual touch because I stupidly made love to her.

"I'm going to clean up." I climb out of bed and shut the bathroom door behind me.

After I wipe off my dick, I stare at myself in the mirror. I couldn't have fucked her on the counter? Doggie style over the love seat? Reverse cowgirl it? I had to do missionary and stare into her eyes the whole time. Her skin felt like silk. I close my eyes, remembering how good she felt under me.

Don't flip out. Be present. This isn't anything. So what? You care for her. Of course the sex can be slow with longing looks and savored tastes. It's all good.

I walk out with a washcloth and sit on the edge of the bed, handing it to her. She puts it between her legs and disappears into the bathroom herself.

Pulling on my pants, I stare out the window at the path

toward the lake. She surprised me when she followed me, and something about her hugging me pulled me to bring her back here. But now I made the mistake of making this something she doesn't want. Even if she thinks she does, she doesn't understand my demons, my inability to really get close to anyone by opening myself up to get hurt.

The bathroom door opens and her gaze falls to my jeans. She picks up her clothes and gets dressed without saying a word.

I snag my shirt off the floor. "I should go."

"Oh. Okay." She sits down on the bed.

"We don't have all the stuff for duo night, and I should, um... get that set for us."

"Yeah, sure. I understand." She nods.

"But this was nice, huh?"

"Nice?" She looks annoyed.

I stand and she doesn't.

Just be straight with her.

"You know what I mean." I smile and bend down, giving her a kiss. I allow myself to savor it, pressing my lips to hers until it's creepy. Her hand is midair as if she was about to put it on my cheek, but I step back. "I'll call you later."

"Yeah, sure."

I look back at her on the bed and give her a small wave, opening the door and leaving. Once I'm on the other side of the door, I release a breath and jog down the steps, away from my demons.

"WHAT ARE YOU TALKING ABOUT? Presley's gonna be here in ten minutes," Jed says when I grab my keys.

"I'll be back before it's over, but I have to go."

I'm not proud of my actions, but after that day with Presley, I bolted and haven't looked back.

"Don't do this, Cade." Jed grabs my shirt, but I shrug him off.

"I told you I have to go. Grandma needs me."

I walk out the back door and run smack into Presley coming in, almost making her drop all her stuff.

"Oh, hey," she says, and her gaze goes right to the ground.

Probably because I've given her the brush-off for the past three days—saying I had to take Rylan to the doctor, or that I was busy with work and errands. All lame, which meant I had to find a new place to hang out since Presley and I are neighbors at both work and home.

"Sorry, Jed's going to handle the meeting. I gotta run." I touch her elbow and kiss her cheek. She turns her head at the last minute and our lips connect. There's that spark that never seems to die, even when I'm being a total ass. Instead of sliding my tongue in as I normally would, I break the kiss and step back. "I'm sure one of you can catch me up on the plans."

"Is everything okay? We could reschedule."

I walk toward my truck, waving. "No. Don't do that."

I climb into my truck, start the ignition, and pull out of the lot without looking back. I'm not sure I could handle seeing the disappointment in her eyes right now. Driving away from the brewery, I release a breath and slam my fist into the steering wheel. What the hell is wrong with me?

Unsure where to go right now, I head to Lake Starlight, needing a different town where no one is watching my every move. After parking my truck, I enter a bar named Lucky's and sit down at the bar. I ask for a whiskey. I think

I'm maybe more than a few deep when Adam and Jed appear, each put an arm under mine, and walk me out of the bar.

"You're fucking lucky Liam from Smokin' Guns knows Fisher so well. He called him to say his brother was drunk and Nate from Lucky's was refusing to serve him anymore," Jed says.

All I really hear is blah, blah, blah. The guy loves to hear the sound of his own voice.

"I'm fine." I shrug out of their hold, but they both have me good and I get nowhere. A gurgling churns in my stomach and I'm pretty sure... yep. "I'm gonna be—"

I throw up right beside a tree.

"Oh look, the same as Savannah back in the day," a man says to his red-haired wife as they walk by.

"She looked prettier doing it." The woman laughs and he bends to kiss her.

"For sure."

She slaps him. "Seriously, Colton, how did we not learn from them?"

They continue walking and I stare on at how happy they are—until another explosion of vomit races up my throat.

A guy comes out of the bar and hands Jed a water.

"I should make you suffer." Jed opens the bottle and hands it to me.

I gulp down half the bottle and sigh. I haven't gotten drunk in fucking ages.

"Take my truck, Adam. I'll drive him home in his," Jed says.

"Why?" Adam asks.

"Because when he pukes again, it'll be in his own truck."

We drive home as Jed continues to lecture me about addressing my issues. He goes on and on about how I'm being ridiculous when it comes to Presley, but I don't wanna hear it.

"Okay, mister one-night stand." I roll down the window for some air. It runs through my hair and I get why dogs do this. It feels like heaven. Not like when I'm deep in Presley, but nice.

I cringe when I think the word nice. I can't believe I said that to her after we had sex.

"We're not the same. We have two very different fucked-up problems. And I don't have one-night stands, I just don't do relationships. It's different."

"And I don't either."

"You do. You've been in a relationship with Presley for however long you've been messing around with her. You're just pretending you're not and torturing yourself in the process."

"You have no idea what you're talking about," I say. He slams on the brakes and I fly forward, hitting my head on the dashboard. I hold my head. "Jackass."

"Still haven't come to your senses yet, huh? Should I slam them again?" He does, but this time I'm prepared and get my hand on the dash before my head slams into it.

"Ha," I say, and he waves me off.

We pull into the driveway and I see that her light is on. Jed puts the truck in park, and I stare at the window.

"I'll see you later," I say.

"Don't go up there tonight," he says and exits the truck.

I open my door and hop out, and Adam almost runs me over when he drives up in Jed's truck. I step back fast. "He almost killed me."

"No, he didn't." Jed is there, blocking the stairs to go up to Presley's.

"Come on. I want to go up there," I whine.

"Why? One reason other than sex," Jed asks, crossing his arms.

Adam tugs on my shirt. "Let her be tonight."

Do they know something I don't? "What am I missing?"

"If you're going up there for a piece of ass, you gotta turn around and go home. Shower, sober up, and see her in the morning," Adam says.

"What? Did something happen?" I step closer, but Jed pushes his chest into mine and I fall back onto my ass.

"Just tell me," I say to Adam.

He looks at me then at Jed before his gaze lands back on me. "You might've ruined your chance. You really hurt her."

"How... I mean, she told you that?"

"Everyone knows. Where the hell have you been the last few days?" Jed yells, not moving from his bodyguard stance.

"Are you fucking her now?" I say to him.

Jed narrows his eyes and outright glares at me. "We're not going through this again. She doesn't want me, and I think I have a proven track record that I don't take your girl."

"She's really not mine," I sulk.

"She could've been, but you fucking ruined it."

God, can Jed just chill the fuck out for a hot second? So I flipped out for a few days.

"Come on, let's get you cleaned up. Nothing good is gonna come from you going up there now." Adam nudges me toward our house.

I look one more time at her door, but what my brothers

are saying make sense. Tomorrow I'll make amends with her.

I'm not in my house for five minutes before I crash face-first on my bed and pass out.

Chapter Thirty-eight

"I knew the stakes and the game I was playing."
-Presley Knight

Presley

The shop door opens and my mom rushes in, her arms wide open. She wraps them around me and squeezes so tight, you'd think I'd been declared missing.

"Hey, Mom," I say.

She draws back and places her hands on my upper arms. "What? What happened?"

I shake my head. "Nothing. Just nerves."

Lie. Lie. Lie.

The fact is, tonight is the duo night and I've done all the planning with Jed. Cade has made excuse after excuse not to come to the meetings. I'm not an idiot—he's dodging me after we made love. I almost offered him an out right after I came out of the bathroom and he had his pants on. But I'm done with that. If he wants to break it off, he can come here and tell me himself.

"Is this about the boy?"

"What boy?" I stopped telling my mom about boys after

Lincoln because I realized I didn't want her opinion to tarnish my own.

"That Cade boy you were always talking about. He owns the brewery, right?"

I guess I divulged more than I thought I did. "He does. We're doing a duo night with them tonight. It's a big thing in this town." I pick up one of the beer-and-books markers Jed had made that says which beer goes with which book.

"Oh, this is cute. I should do this for the girls in my book club except it would have to be with wine."

I get the impression there's more wine than books going on at her book club, but I guess when your child grows up, you have to find something to do with your time.

I circle around with my arms open. "So what do you think?"

I would love to say my mother's opinion of my store doesn't matter, but it does.

She walks around and picks up a book here and there. Touches the wall the apple tree is painted on. Smiles at the toadstools. Frowns at the young adult section. When I hit thirteen, my mom feared how much books could teach me about boys. But that's still my favorite genre to read.

"It's cute. You did a great job. I knew you would."

Then I realize that my dad still hasn't come in. I thought maybe he was parking the car or something. "Where's Dad?"

She sets her purse on the counter, near the cash register. "He sends his apologies. He had to work. You know how it is."

I really don't, but it's the same excuse she always gives when it comes to him. "Oh, okay."

"But he wanted me to tell you how proud of you he is. I think you'll be getting a special delivery tomorrow." She winks, which means a giant bouquet is on its way. It's his go-to move. My dad should invest in growers with the amount of flowers he has to send every year.

"I'm sure I'll love them."

She winds her arm through mine. "Do we need to do anything beforehand?"

I look around. "I think I'm ready."

I could use a bottle of vodka to calm my nerves before I unlock those doors and welcome all of Sunrise Bay. I'm not gonna lie, I wish Cade was here with me, but clearly whatever we were is over.

"Then show me the town," she says as though Sunrise Bay is Disney World.

"Yeah. Want to do lunch?"

"Not at the brewery though, right?"

Although they have great food, I am not entering that establishment until I have to. "Nope. We'll find somewhere else. A lot of the places on the bay have opened up now that tourist season is almost here."

She pats my hand. "I can't wait to spend the day with you."

She beams, seeming like she's genuinely on cloud nine with me. She tried for years for a child and always says I was her blessing, her answered prayer. This might be the first time in a long time that I'm really *feeling* it though and it took me coming here for it to happen.

As we step out of the store and I lock it, Cade is crossing the road from The Grind, a drink in his hand. He looks horrible. When he glances over, he stops. Mom's too busy chatting about how the town looks like a place Dad took her up in Vermont to notice.

My eyes lock with Cade's, and I wish more than anything that I knew what made him do a one-eighty with me. What scared him away? I wish he could talk to me about it.

I turn my mom in the other direction and I don't look back because as it is, I'm sucking back tears. Where did it all go wrong in such a short amount of time? But my breakdown will have to wait. Right now, I'm going to enjoy the time with someone who wants to be with me.

CLARA BITES her lip and nods. "Do it."

I unlock the door and she claps. My mom is busy rearranging the kids' section because she said I should put my most loved books from when I was younger, front and center. I watch while the people of Sunrise Bay walk into my new store for the first time.

"Now you can sample the beers over at Truth or Dare, but we both have the bundles of the beer and books to purchase," I announce, but everyone is looking around and they don't seem to pay much attention.

Clara elbows me. "Everything's going great. A few old ladies are in the romance section, pretending to be lost."

I'm not surprised that I recognize them from the Northern Lights Retirement Center.

A few customers ask me for specific books, telling me they love that I'll be just down the street. Others ask me about special orders and if they can place a request. A woman approaches me about starting a book club one night a month because she loves discussing books but none of her friends like to read what she does.

Everything is going great. Midway through the night, the crowd dwindles because I'm sure most of them are congregated over in Truth or Dare—hopefully buying more books and beer. Jed said it's important that we sell a lot tonight, that there's some kind of bragging rights for the two companies that earn the most.

"Seems everyone loves your store." Mom comes alongside me as I'm checking a woman out.

"I think so."

"Now you just have to hope it continues and it's not a one-night thing."

My mom can be pessimistic when it comes to something that's working against her. And The Story Shop succeeding is definitely working against her because it means I'll stay here.

Over the years, I've learned not to fight with her but go with the flow. No need to rile her up when nothing is final. "I hope so."

Her hand runs down my back. "You did a great job. I'm going to head next door and check out what they're doing to drive business here."

"Really?" I ask because a brewery is not my mom's scene.

"Well, I want to make sure they're showing off your books just as much as they are their beer."

Clara smiles from across the room.

"Clara, do you want to take her over there?" I ask.

She sets down the book in her hand. "Sure. Come on, Mrs. Knight. You might like one of the beers."

"Oh no, I do *not* drink beer." My mom looks at Clara for a moment. She hasn't yet addressed the fact that Clara's my biological sister. I'm pretty sure it's Mom's way of pretending it's not happening. "If you had blonde hair, the two of you would be spitting images of one another."

Clara glances at me over my mom's shoulder in surprise, and I'm sure I match her expression.

I waggle my eyebrows at Clara. "Maybe you should go blonde."

"I did, about a decade ago. Too much maintenance," she says with a smile.

"Truth. Maybe I should go brunette."

My mom's head whips in my direction and she gives a small shake of her head. That's the difference between Clara and me. Where I grew up, you don't leave your house without a full face of makeup, dressed to impress. Anything natural isn't the norm, hence my blonde hair. I'm starting to think maybe it's time for a change though.

"We'll be right back." Clara leads my mom out of the store, and they veer left through the crowd of people outside.

Then I spot Cade in the crowd. He's a little taller than the people he's with, but he's got a beer in his hand. Again I question what went wrong with us. I thought a friendship was growing between us. I admit I caught feelings, but I wasn't going to tell him that or pressure him to make it something more.

My thoughts are interrupted when the bell rings again and Ethel, Dori, and Midge walk in.

"Parsley," Ethel says, coming over while Dori and Midge walk around and check things out.

I don't bother correcting her on the name thing—I'm sure she'll only deny it again. I've yet to put in security cameras and I really hope that Midge doesn't help herself.

As though Ethel sees me watching Midge, she pats my hand. "Dori will keep an eye on her." Her gaze scatters around the store. "It's beautiful. You did a great job."

"Thank you."

"I already bought the summer read and six-pack from next door. I'm giving the beer to Sal down at Northern

Lights. They tell him he shouldn't drink beer, but I sneak it into him."

I really hope when I'm older, I live somewhere like Northern Lights. Those elderly people are probably having more fun than high school kids.

"Well, thank you for supporting duo night."

She smiles and pats my hand. "Now tell me why my grandson is out there looking so depressed." She nods toward where I saw Cade before she came in.

"I'm not sure."

"Is what Nikki's saying true? You two are over?"

I choke out a laugh. "We never even began."

"Oh, that's not true and we both know it."

The door chimes again and of course it's Reese who walks in, along with a woman carrying a baby to her chest.

"Grandma Ethel!" Reese coos and prances over in her high heels with her arms out.

But the truth is, I've never been so happy to see Reese. Her arrival means an end to this conversation with Ethel.

"Reese," Ethel says in a frigid tone but does hug her.

"I missed you so much."

"Funny, I never got a card. Or a call." She winds her arm through mine. "Have you met Presley Knight, Sunrise Bay's newest resident?"

Reese smiles. Man, she'd give the girls back in Connecticut a run for their money. "I did."

"So you know that she and Cade are—"

The girl with the baby rolls her eyes and heads to the children's section. I wish I could follow her. I glance around and catch Dori smacking Midge's hand.

"Oh, Cade just told me they're just friends," Reese says.

"You know Cade," Ethel says.

"He keeps those feelings to himself," she says. "I know, I

still remember when he finally opened up to me about his mom."

Ethel glances at me from the corner of her eye and I swear it feels as if someone used a pair of tweezers and pulled the realization out of the back of my head. What the hell? How did I not put everything together? This whole time I thought Cade's inability to open up to me had to do with Reese but it was actually about the loss of his mom.

"It was a hard loss for him, and I don't think we should all be gossiping about it," Ethel says.

By Reese's twisted face, she's just as surprised as I am that any subject is off the table to gossip about with Ethel.

"Definitely." But Reese's smug look that says Cade's shared more with her than he ever will with me sets my teeth on edge. God help me, I'm still jealous. Another bad sign. "I should join my friend. Sorry it didn't work out, Presley. Cade is the bachelor of Sunrise Bay, but he only trusts a few people."

As if by speaking his name she made him appear, the door chimes and Cade walks in.

I can't deal with this right now. It's all too overwhelming. My chest feels tight and my heart is racing and all I can think of is bolting.

"I'm sorry, I need a breather. Can you watch the store?" Leaving it with Ethel isn't the best option, but my throat is closing up. There's no way I'm talking to him right now.

Reese catches him first and beelines over to him, hugging him tightly. I walk toward the door.

Cade dislodges himself from Reese. "Presley, wait."

But I don't stop. I push the shop door open, almost hitting a man. "Sorry," I say and walk away from the crowd congregated outside our businesses.

"Presley!" Cade yells, and a deafening silence falls over the crowd.

I turn around, exhausted. "What?"

"Let's talk." He follows me in the direction of The Grind.

"You've had time to talk, Cade."

He shoves his hands in his pockets and stares at his feet. He doesn't really want to talk.

"See? You can't talk. Isn't that the problem?" Unshed tears prick at my eyes and I hold them back, doing my best not to lose my shit right here in front of everyone. I thought the town would break me, but it was him. Anger and frustration stack up inside me and I stand straighter. I cross my arms and wait. "Okay, you want to talk? Talk."

"Let's go somewhere else."

I look behind him at all the faces staring at us. "Why? Everyone here knows what's going on with us." I look around him at all the townspeople. "Yes, Nikki was right. Cade and I have been screwing for the past few weeks."

A few people laugh, some look on with sympathy, but I don't care.

I put up my hand. "Maybe I should clarify. We weren't screwing. We were messing around until a week ago when he made love to me."

He looks up and the shame on his face breaks me. A tear slips down my cheek and he steps forward, but I swipe it away, stepping back.

"Presley," he says.

I shake my head. "Don't sweat it, Cade, I was just as naïve as you. I knew the stakes and the game I was playing. But I'm done. So you don't have to gently break my heart by dodging me anymore. I'm giving you the out you're looking for."

He steps forward again, and my head falls down to hide the tears that won't seem to stop cascading down my cheeks.

"Come on. Let's talk." He reaches to touch me and I smack his hand away.

"You had your chance to talk to me. It's too late now."

"It's not. I'm here."

"Okay, why did you run out after you made love to me?"

He opens his mouth and closes it, shaking his head. "I got scared."

"Of?" I break the small distance between us. If he's willing to open up, I'll go somewhere with him and talk this out. But if he's not, then there's no point.

"Because I didn't want you to get the wrong idea. I got scared that I hurt you."

A stabbing sensation pierces my chest. "So there are no feelings on your side? I was just a girl to mess around with?"

He looks down again and nods.

All the air rushes from my lungs. I nod and close my eyes, gathering all the strength I have left. "Thanks for finally being honest. Have a good life."

I walk past him toward my store. The crowd acts as if they weren't hanging on our every word and goes back to their conversations.

"Presley!" Cade calls. "I'm sorry."

"Don't be. You saved me a lot of trouble." I meet Reese and her smirk outside The Story Shop, but I push past her.

Then I head to the back room and sink down in my office chair, wishing I'd never tried to have a fresh start.

Chapter Twenty-nine

"Son, you're stronger than this."
-Hank Greene

Cade

Three days after the grand opening of The Story Shop, four days after Presley decided to have it out with me in the middle of duo night with the entire town as our witness, I'm at my mom's gravesite.

What a fantastic fucking week this is turning out to be.

Chevelle hands us all flowers, each one different to make a bouquet that Mom would love. She always said she never had a favorite flower, how could she choose, they're all beautiful like her kids. But I might be the only one who remembers Mom saying that. Sometimes I think being the oldest child with the clearest memories of her is a curse.

"We'll start oldest to youngest, like always," Chevelle says, nodding at me.

I blow out a breath, not really into this. "I'll pass right now."

"Cade, you always go first," she says.

I shake my head. I don't want to do the rah-rah talk to make all my siblings feel better. We've all lived without her longer than we lived with her. There's nothing rah-rah about how I'm feeling right now, and I only have myself to blame.

I let Presley slip through my hands. I lied to her when I said I felt nothing. She was right to call me out.

"Not this year." I place the lily in the vase next to Mom's grave. I wonder if Chevelle planned the lily because of the ceramic lily Presley painted at Fired Up. I never did ask if it was her favorite or not. Because I knew I was sinking farther and farther into her and I thought if I knew less about her, it would make it easier to stay afloat.

"Okay, fine. Fisher." Chevelle motions to him.

Fisher clears his throat and gives his usual few words about missing her and don't worry, he's keeping Sunrise Bay safe. Xavier talks about his season and the fact he's starting next season. He wishes her a happy birthday and drops his tulip in the vase. Adam wipes his face, probably wishing he could listen to some Motown to push aside any feelings. He apologizes for his marriage not working out. That he didn't do what it took to make it work and he's sorry he's disappointed her since she and Dad were college sweethearts.

"Adam, Mom wouldn't care. All she'd want is for you to be happy," I say. He shouldn't feel guilty that he and Lucy didn't work out.

"She would've wanted you to be happy too," he says and slides his rose into the vase.

"I am happy."

Fisher blows out a breath.

"What?" I ask.

"Nothing. I'm tired," he says.

"My turn." Chevelle stands straight and pulls a piece of paper from her purse. "I wanted to write Mom a poem, but turns out it's the one thing I'm not good at."

We all laugh. I wish I would've had her read it to me that day in the kitchen. Another fail for me.

"But I wrote a letter."

Fisher groans. I know he's not into these days. He'd rather deal with this on his own, same as me. He's just more vocal about it.

"'Mom, I'm sorry...'" She glances up, and all of us huddle around her because we know the guilt that weighs heavily on her small shoulders. Our mom's death is not her fault like she thinks it is. She was five. She didn't know. "'But we have a problem. Because you died, Cade is scared.'"

I draw back, and Fisher's gaze meets mine.

"'He's scared to get close to someone. I'm sure you know, but there's this new woman in town, Presley.'"

Adam steps back, smiling at our sister for calling me out.

"'He's so happy when he's with her, Mom. I'm sure you see his smile all the way in heaven. But he's trying to act like he doesn't care about her. He humiliated her in front of the whole town. I know, I know. Not very Greene-like.'" She scolds me with a glare. "'Please do whatever you can to reach him and send him a message that he can't turn the clock back to before she came into town. Those feelings he has for her are never going to go away. If anything, he'll hate himself when he finally realizes he lost her when he's sitting at her wedding as a guest.'"

All my siblings stare at me.

I hold up my hand. "Is this some kind of bullshit intervention?"

Chevelle puts her hands on Mom's headstone. "'Thanks, Mom. We love you and not a day goes by that I don't think about you.'" She drops a daisy in the vase. "Happy birthday."

I stalk down to my truck, shaking my head, upset that a day we came to remember our mom has turned into something focused on me.

"Cade!" Chevelle runs after me and grasps my elbow. "It's okay to put yourself out there."

I turn back around to find all my siblings standing with Chevelle.

"We all feel the pain," Xavier says. "None of us want to feel it again, but we can't just stop living."

"I'm surviving after Lucy," Adam says. "I'm here and her leaving devastated me."

"You guys were too young to understand," I say.

"I'm only two years younger than you," Fisher says. "It hurts, yeah, but you can love someone again."

"I've seen you two together," Adam says. "You've already fallen in love with her whether you want to admit it or not."

My dad's truck pulls up behind mine. He always joins us a few minutes after we start in case we want to say something we don't want him to hear.

"What's going on?" he asks as he walks over to us.

I cross my arms. "Seems my siblings earned psychology degrees I didn't know about. They have a lot of opinions about why it didn't work out with Presley."

Dad sighs and pats my siblings on the shoulders. "Give us a minute," he says to them.

"We'll be at the house," Xavier says.

Marla is making a huge meal at the house like she usually does after we've done our graveside visit.

Chevelle hugs me with tears in her eyes. "I'm sorry if you're angry, but I can't let you ruin your chance at happiness."

I hug her tightly and pass her to Fisher, who walks her over to his truck.

"Walk with me," my dad says.

I follow, expecting him to go back up to my mom's grave, but he heads the opposite way.

"When your mom died, I never thought I'd love again. I didn't want to put you guys through having a stepmom, and I wasn't quite sure I could open myself up to caring like that for someone again. But when Marla returned, we just fit."

I say nothing and keep walking, kicking at the leaves that were left behind under the melted snow.

"Don't take this the wrong way, but having Marla in my life was worth putting you guys through a huge change. I'd forgotten what it was like to have a partner. Someone to listen to you, give you advice, or just love you. Someone you knew would have your back at all costs. I felt empty, and though I could stand it, once Marla came and filled that emptiness, I knew what I'd been missing. As scared as I was of going through a loss like I did with your mother's death, I didn't want to turn away because I understood that my life would be better with Marla in it."

"Yeah, but you and Marla liked each other in high school. You already had feelings for her."

He sighs and glances at me as if I'm grasping at straws. "I did like Marla in high school, but when I met your mother, I fell head over heels in love with her. You loved Reese in high school. Do you feel the same for her now?"

"You know, I don't think I really did love her, looking back now. If I did, it was teenage love. Not all-consuming adult love."

"I was scared to love someone again, to open myself to the devastation I felt when your mom died. But I got through it once. If I had to do it again, I could. So could you." Dad gestures toward all the gravestones. "All of these people lived life. Some had their lives cut too short, like your mother. Some lived until they were a hundred. The problem is, you get one life and you have no idea how long it will be. You might as well live it. Some things work out how you hope, and some don't. Even if it doesn't work out how you want, that doesn't mean it's not worth doing."

He stops at a gravestone. It reads Benjamin Oliver and I calculate the birth to death dates, figuring out he was only eighteen when he died.

Dad says, "I went to high school with Benny."

The name Benny rings a bell. A car crash, I think.

"I always think about what he missed out on, dying so young. He never got married, had the blessing of having kids, seeing them grow up, watching them make bad decisions." He raises his eyebrows at me. "It puts things in perspective. You can be dead and not living, but you can also be alive and not living too." He pats me on the shoulder. "I'm going to wish your mom a happy birthday. See you back at the house."

He leaves me standing in front of Benny's grave.

———

I DRIVE over to Marla and my dad's house, leaving my dad at Mom's gravesite. He's probably complaining about me to her too.

The driveway is filled with all my siblings' and stepsiblings' cars.

I hear laughter in the kitchen when I walk in the house, a noise I'm so accustomed to here—a noise that never would've been here had Marla not entered our lives. Sure, we were happy before her, but she brought something special, as did each of my stepsiblings. Had my dad not taken that chance, my life now would be very different. Marla's even helped Chevelle work through some of her guilt. I could never repay her for that.

The room quiets with my entrance. All of my stepsiblings come over and hug me.

Jed slaps me on the back. "Come to your senses at all?"

I ignore the jab. "When did you become Team Presley?"

He shrugs. "I like her. And Books and Beers made the most money on duo night, so... bragging rights."

Marla hugs me tightly, her hand running up and down my back. "You okay?"

I nod. "Yep, if everyone would stay out of my business."

The whole room erupts into a conversation of how this big family is in everyone's business, not just mine.

"Would you mind setting the table?" Marla asks.

"Sure."

She picks up a stack of plates and hands them to me. I go to the dining room and see that all the leaves are already in the table, making it stretch the entire length of the large room. I place all the plates down, but run out before I reach the final chair. Huh.

"Marla, we have one extra chair," I call.

She's mixing the salad and her smile dims. "Oh, yeah, sorry."

"Is someone else coming?"

She shakes her head. "No, you can take it away. I thought someone might be joining us." She sighs and goes back to mixing her salad.

"Who?"

All my siblings and stepsiblings groan.

"How on Earth are you the oldest?" Nikki asks.

"What am I missing?"

Chevelle steps over to me with an exasperated expression. "The speech and the letter were supposed to put some sense into your brain to make up with Presley. The chair is for Presley!" She throws her arms in the air. "It's a lost cause. He's going to die alone."

Tears spring from Chevelle's eyes and Marla is quick to hug her.

"I'm not gonna die alone. Jed will be next to me," I say, but no one laughs.

Jed finishes swallowing a pull from his beer. "Hell no. I'm not wiping your ass."

At least one person in this room is willing to joke about this.

"At least Mom lived a good life. She had five kids, she was happy and in love. Your looks aren't going to last forever," Adam says.

"Dad's still looking good," I counter.

"Seriously?" Chevelle asks.

Marla puts up her hands to stop us all from fighting. "This is Cade's decision, everyone. We've all interjected ourselves enough at this point. We tried and failed."

"You mean you all planned this entire thing? On Mom's birthday?" I ask.

They all nod. Everyone is in on it.

"We love you and we want you to be happy," Chevelle says.

I hug her. "I am happy."

She shakes her head against my chest. "Not as happy as you were with Presley."

My dad walks in and frowns—from seeing me here alone, I guess.

"Okay, let's eat," Marla announces.

Everyone takes a dish and heads to the dining room. Dad lingers with Marla, hugging her and kissing her forehead. I hear them whisper I love yous and Marla asking Dad if he's okay. He only holds her a little tighter.

I go back to the dining room. I'm about to sit down when Nikki pulls her vibrating phone from her pocket. She glances at me then responds to the text.

"One of your many sources?" I ask.

"Oh, this is something you'll want to know."

"Doubt it," I say, my hand on the back of my chair.

"Turns out Presley is booked on a flight back to Connecticut tonight. Looks like you got your wish, Cade. She's out of your life permanently."

I snatch her phone and she tries to grab it back, but I put my palm on her head to keep her in her seat, holding the phone high. I see who her source is, and damn, I'm surprised and annoyed at the same time. But the source is legit, so I hand it back to her.

"You cannot tell a soul," she says, warning me with her finger.

Everyone looks at me as Dad and Marla walk in.

"This is your last chance. You really gonna let her go?" Jed asks.

A reel of my time with her runs through my mind.

"Son, you're stronger than this." Dad puts his hand on my shoulder. "It takes a strong heart to love again."

"Ah, Hank, no worries. I'll take Presley off his hands." Jed stands and drops the napkin on the table.

Just the thought of Presley with Jed or anyone else makes the arteries in my neck pop out. I couldn't stand that.

"Finally!" Jed's head falls back. "All it took was some good ol' jealousy."

"I'll be back."

Unfortunately, Jed's right. I'm an idiot.

"Where is she?" I ask Nikki.

She hammers a message out on her phone to her "source." "She's at the apartment above the garage, cleaning it out."

I race out of Dad and Marla's house and jump into my truck. I can't let her leave this all behind. Leave me behind. I might be slow on the uptake, but I'm going to do everything in my power to make Presley see what everyone else already has—we're meant to be together.

Chapter Thirty

"Will you go on a walk with me?"
-Cade Greene

Presley

My mom is leaving tonight, but she's helping me clean out the apartment before she goes.

She comes out of the bathroom. "Bathroom is done."

She holds up the black trash bags full of my rugs, shower curtain, and toiletry items. The fact she's willing to help with this says how much she loves me. She sits on the bed I've already stripped, the one that started this whole mess with Cade.

"Sweetie, come home with me," she says.

I shake my head, throwing away the food that's about to expire and I don't want to take with me. I found a small place to rent closer to town, where I can walk to work. The rental car was getting expensive, so I bought a cheap one to get me by for a while.

I'm not proud of my actions with Cade. There's no excuse for me hashing it out with the entire town watching. Maybe I was trying to hurt him as much as he hurt me, I don't know.

"I can't. I have the bookstore."

"But he's going to be right next to you."

I dump the cream cheese. "I know."

"You'll still be neighbors, even if you don't live here." She looks around. It's clear from her cringe she doesn't think much of the apartment. But like all the Greene children, I'll always hold memories of this place near to my heart.

Cade might not be ready to admit what he felt for me. I have no control over that. Maybe I should have pressed more. Maybe I shouldn't have pressed at all, I don't know. Another woman might have gotten him to open up. But I thought with time... I shake my head to stop myself from overthinking. It's over and all I can do is deal with it and try to move on.

"I came to this town for Clara too."

"So you're never coming home?" There's a hitch in my mom's voice.

I close the fridge, sit on the bed, and take her hands. "Mom, I love you. Thank you for always being my biggest cheerleader. I don't want you to think me coming here is to get away from you. I'd love if you and Dad would relocate here. But this is the first place I feel like myself. I feel like I really fit, despite the recent drama."

"Did I make a mistake raising you in Connecticut?"

I lean my head on her shoulder. "You and Dad gave me a great life. And maybe it's my genes, why I love it here so much. Maybe it has nothing to do with biology. But I'm happy here in a way I wasn't in Connecticut."

"Even though that boy broke your heart?"

"That's the good thing with broken hearts—they heal." *Eventually.*

She kisses my forehead. "I'm not sure when you became the wise one."

"As soon as you held me in your arms."

She pushes me away with her shoulder and laughs. "I'm going to come visit a lot. You'll need a spare room. And even though that Cade fella missed his chance, the next guy from this town who's worthy of winning your heart, he's gonna have to get used to me."

I put my arm around her. "I'd have it no other way."

"I might talk your dad into getting a place here for when we visit. We could rent it out when we're not in town. It'd be a good investment." She winks.

I chuckle, knowing that will be a selling point to him. "I'd love that."

She pats her hand on my shoulder. "I'm only a flight away."

"I know."

She sighs and our heads touch, the two of us deep in thought. This might be the hardest thing my mom has ever had to do, and I'm proud of her for taking it so well. She wouldn't always have been so graceful about accepting my decision.

The sound of tires on gravel interrupts our moment.

"Clara told me they have a big family dinner, that no one would be around." I stand and look out the curtain. A boulder sinks into my stomach when I see Cade's truck park and him getting out of it. "It's Cade."

Then we hear his footsteps on the wooden stairs outside the apartment and a loud knock sounds on the door.

My mom pats my knee. "I'll handle this."

She walks over to the door while I shut myself in the bathroom. Sooner or later, I'll have to face him, but not right now.

"Hello, Cade," she says.

"Hello, Mrs. Knight. I don't think we officially met the other night. I'm Cade Greene."

"Oh, I know who you are."

"I suppose you do. Is Presley here?"

There's a pause. "She is, but she's not here for you. You've done enough."

I hear a hand land on the door. "Please. I just need a few minutes. That's all. I'm an idiot."

"You are," Mom says, and I bite my lip to keep from laughing.

"I love your daughter. Please let me tell her."

I suck in a sharp breath.

"Cade—" she says.

"Presley!" he yells into the apartment. "Please talk to me. I love you. I know I've been so stupid, but if you give me ten minutes, I'll explain it all. And if you still hate me and want nothing to do with me, then I'll drive to the airport."

What is he talking about? Why would he drive to the airport?

My hand wraps around the doorknob.

"I'm sure you're a good man, but sometimes things can't be mended. And in truth, if you didn't realize you loved my daughter until you lost her, I'm not sure I'm on board with you talking to her now."

"I'll gladly explain myself to you too. My mom died when I was twelve and—"

I turn the knob and step out. His shoulders deflate when he sees me. He tries to get around my mom, but she steps in front of him, her hand on his chest.

I want to laugh. "It's okay, Mom."

She turns around and steps aside. "Presley."

There's a warning in her tone, but I want to at least hear him out.

"Will you go on a walk with me?" He holds out his hand. "You're welcome to come, Mrs. Knight."

"No." She steps back farther. "You two go."

She puts her hand on my shoulder and kisses my cheek as though she wants to give me the strength she thinks I need. And she'd be right.

I step out of the apartment.

"We won't be gone long," he says to my mom and shuts the door.

I walk down the stairs and his hand slides around mine, but I slide mine back out. I'm not ready for that.

"The day you found me out by the lake, I was remembering my mom." He leads us down the path through the woods. "I already knew you weren't just a friend with benefits by then. It wasn't like I was hit over the head with it and opened my eyes one day and realized I wanted to be more than just friends with you. It was gradual. That day, I was scared to have sex with you because I didn't know what would happen. And then I ended up making love to you. Maybe part of me wanted to know how that would feel because I knew I was going to bail." He shakes his head as we come to the clearing of the lake.

"I don't understand. I get that neither of us wanted a relationship, but after the feelings developed, we didn't really have a choice."

He stares out at the lake. "My mom drowned in this lake."

My eyes close. "I'm so sorry."

"I know. Everyone is. I was twelve, and my dad had us all at football practice. Chevelle was home with my mom.

She thought we were all outside having fun skating on the lake and she snuck out. She was always chasing us around, wanting to play with her older brothers. Mom ran out to get her when she realized she was gone, and when she got here, Chevelle was standing in the middle of the frozen lake. We'd just returned from football and saw my mom running to the lake. She yelled to my dad and we all followed."

I take his hand. "You don't have to tell me this. It's okay."

He looks at me, tears glistening in his eyes. "I do. Because I love you and I want you to know why I struggled to accept my feelings." His Adam's apple bobs when he swallows. "Mom got across the ice and told Chevelle to come back to my dad. As soon as my sister was safe... that's when the ice splintered. By the time my dad got to her, it was too late."

I tighten my grip. "Oh, Cade."

He nods. "It was so long ago." He blinks and his eyes start to clear as he widens them and sniffs to stop the tears from falling. "I'm scared. I'm scared that if I admit these feelings I have for you and let myself sink into them, there's a chance that I could lose you. I don't want to feel that kind of pain again."

I walk into his arms and hold him tightly. This was Marla's cryptic message. I knew it had to do with his mom, but it's amazing how it all fits now that I have all the pieces.

"I'm sorry, Presley. For putting you through all that. I never planned on falling in love with you, but I did, and I'd be a fucking fool to let you go. I finally realized that it doesn't hurt any less losing you this way than if we were together and something happened." He takes me by the shoulders and pushes me out of his embrace so that he can meet my gaze. "If you want to go home to Connecticut, I understand. I embarrassed you, and I promise to make it up to you. If there's still a chance... I can't go tonight, but I'll square things away here and meet you there. That is, if you'll have me."

I place my hands on his stubbled cheeks. "I've got a tougher skin than you give me credit for. I'm not going anywhere. I like Sunrise Bay."

"But Nikki said—"

I shake my head. "Nope."

"So you're staying?"

I nod.

"Can you forgive me?" He looks as if he's holding his breath, waiting for my response.

"All I ever wanted was for you to be honest with me. I understand you're scared. I am too. But we can navigate through all of it together. You just have to let me in."

"You're in. You're already in my heart. I'm not sure I could keep you out no matter how hard I tried."

I rest my chin on his chest, looking up at him. "Then let's do this."

"Rules?" he asks. His hand slides around my neck, his fingers threading through my hair.

I shake my head. "No rules this time."

"Sounds perfect to me."

He dips his head but pauses right before his lips touch mine. "And don't feel like you have to say you love me back. I'll totally wait."

"Once you set everyone in Sunrise Bay straight and declare your love for me, I'll get back to you on the I love you thing. Maybe you can put up a banner downtown or something."

He laughs, tilting his head back.

I grab his shirt and pull him toward me. "I love you too."

His lips fall to mine, and for the first time, all the pieces of my life fit together perfectly. I know it's a fleeting feeling and our road will be bumpy, but as I told him, as long as we're on the ride together, that's good enough for me.

Cade

One year later

"I'm not so sure about this," I say to Clara. I'm just being honest—I don't know if Presley will be cool wearing this ring.

"Believe me, she'll love it. And hello, it's been a year. No more dragging your feet, Cade Greene."

I hold up my hands. "Hey, I've been all in."

And I have been. I'll be the first to admit it took me forever to realize that losing Presley would hurt no matter if I let her slip away now or in fifty years. If I didn't want to love someone, I never should've picked her for a friends with benefits arrangement. It was a losing bet from the get-go.

I ended up moving out of my childhood home, and Presley and I bought a small house on the outskirts of downtown together, close to my parents and close to our businesses. It's actually cheesy how we walk to work together when it's nice, and sometimes on slow days, we walk home for lunch. Wink, wink, if you get what I mean.

"I'm so happy for you guys," Clara says.

Watching not only my own relationship with Presley grow but watching her relationship with Clara grow into a true friendship and sisterhood this past year has been everything. I think it's something they both needed. But still, I'm not sure I can trust Clara on this.

I look at the ring again. "It's a once-in-a-lifetime question. If I fuck this up, it's all she'll remember."

"You're not going to mess it up. Look at this place." She gestures to the ground beyond the deck.

A path of tea lights in luminary bags lead up to the entrance of a teepee with white sheets over it. Inside is a big fluffy blanket and a laptop set up to display the last year of our lives in a slideshow. Thank goodness for Clara's and my family's need to constantly snap pictures. I did have to swear Nikki to silence, which wasn't easy.

"You better go. She's on her way home. Thanks for your help."

"We'll see you at the brewery." She jumps up and down, clapping. Always the cheerleader.

"If she says no, have the whiskey ready."

She hugs me hard. "She's not going to. Welcome to the family."

I shake my head. I'm looking forward to this, but I'll be happy when this is over. It's nerve-racking as hell.

I catch sight of Presley's SUV driving down the road and I push Clara out. She sneaks away through the thick trees. The sun is about to set, so the timing couldn't be more perfect.

I leave the note I prepared on the table before heading outside. Waiting in the teepee is excruciating as I see

Presley turn on the lights in the house. A minute later, she walks out on the balcony and glances down.

"Cade," she says with that smile I love. "What are you up to?"

She walks down the stairs and through the path of luminaries, her eyes locked with mine. She's not stupid, she knows exactly what this is. And I pray her smile means my racing heart can calm down.

When she reaches the teepee, I offer my hand to steady her. "Take off your shoes."

She does and sits on the fluffy blanket. "It's gorgeous."

I lean forward and kiss her. "You're gorgeous." I hand her the laptop and kiss her one more time.

"What did you do?"

"Stop asking questions and press Play."

She does, and a three-minute video of pictures and videos of us this past year plays. Her head falls on my chest and I wrap my arm around her shoulders.

"I love you," she says in the middle, and I point at the screen for her to pay attention.

This section shows our trip to Connecticut so I could meet her dad, which is when I asked him for his daughter's hand. I told him I didn't know when I would propose, but I knew I wanted her to be my wife. We went on a ski trip and headed down to the lower forty-eight to see Xavier play. The rest of the video is filled with kisses my family caught when we didn't know anyone was watching.

At the end, Will You Marry Me? comes on the screen and the music continues.

She turns to me, tears glistening in her eyes.

"I never imagined my life could be this happy. All those years I pushed it away, and I'm glad I did because I think you and I have the perfect love. You're meant for me,

Presley Knight, and I think I'm meant for you. This past year has been amazing. How about we make it last a lifetime?" I pull out the ring, scared to death for this part. I never should have let Clara talk me into this.

"Cade, I'd love to marry you. We are meant for each other." She rises on her knees and kisses me.

"Whoa now, hold on, lady, you gotta wear the ring first."

She giggles and falls back down to her bum.

I offer the silver-banded diamond ring. "This was your Grandma Beatrice's diamond, but I put it in a new setting. Clara thought—"

"I love it," she gushes.

"I have another one picked out if you don't like this," I say, giving her an out.

She shakes her head. "No. She's the one who brought me back here all those years ago. When she died, I met a stranger at a cemetery who would later turn out to be you. It's only fitting that we use her diamond."

I smile, remembering that day I mistook her for Clara.

"That might not have been our time, but fate brought us together again."

"Thank goodness, because I think you saved my life."

She straddles me and I put my hands on the back of her head, threading my fingers through her beautiful blonde hair.

"We saved each other," she says.

She holds her hand out and I slip the ring on her finger. A perfect fit.

"Kiss me, soon-to-be Mrs. Greene?"

"Every day for the rest of my life." Her lips land on mine and my body finally feels at peace.

A HALF HOUR LATER, it's all I can do to get Presley out of the teepee. Thank goodness we had some privacy.

"Do I have to put a bra on?" she asks.

"I wish you didn't, but yes, we're going to be in public." I stand with my hand out.

"Public? Why?"

"Because the first day of tourism season starts tomorrow and we're going to support the town. Plus, I want to show off my new fiancée."

Her hand lands in mine and I pull her up. "Well, when you put it that way."

We walk toward downtown, enjoying the nice spring night.

Everyone from Sunrise Bay has come out. As we approach Truth or Dare, there's a mass of people inside and outside because of the new beer flavor releasing today. Jed took care of it for me. But people walking past the brewery are gawking at the large sign out front.

I love Presley Knight... soon-to-be Presley Greene.

"My declaration of love to you in front of the whole town." I hold out my arms. "Just like you wanted."

"You didn't," Presley says, standing in front of me with her forehead on my chest.

"You want me to put it up in the square instead?"

Clara runs out of the brewery. "So?"

I lift Presley's hand and she turns around.

"She said yes," I say.

Everyone cheers and claps, and Presley turns the most beautiful shade of pink. Then she punches me in the side. "Seriously, talk about embarrassing."

"You're embarrassed by this? All the shit that's been talked about you and the fact that you agreed to be my wife is what embarrasses you?"

She wraps her arms around my stomach. "I love you."

I kiss her forehead, her nose, and her mouth. "I love you. Let's go celebrate. Grandma Ethel is a little upset I'm not using her ring."

I take Presley's hand and we walk into Truth or Dare, thanking everyone for their well wishes. My family is in the corner and soon we're all nestled together, everyone hugging Presley and looking at the ring.

"Finally," Adam says, cuddled up beside his new girl-friend. He's finally moved on and Motown has become go-to music for him, but not just to forget Lucy.

"Better late than never, right?" I say.

He fist bumps me.

The room quiets and I groan, thinking Grandma Ethel has a mic and is about to give a speech that will no doubt be either embarrassing or off-color. I find Presley and bring her in front of me, but everyone in the bar is parting, making a path right to us in the back corner.

"What the hell?" Jed says when a dark-haired woman emerges. "Holy shit."

"Lucy?" Adam says, sounding confused and disbe-lieving.

"Hey, babe, it's nuts out there, right? I forgot how crazy the night before tourist season begins is." She slides between Adam and his girlfriend, kissing him on the cheek.

Holy shit is right.

"That's Lucy?" Presley whispers, and I nod.

"Excuse me. Excuse me." Lucy's mom comes through the crowd next and her hand wraps around Lucy's arm. "Lucy, you can't run off like that." Then she seems to notice who Lucy's with. "I—oh, Adam."

"Susan?" Adam asks, looking between his estranged wife and her mother.

Lucy slides her arm through Adam's again and looks my way. "Oh. I saw the sign. Are you Presley?"

Presley nods.

"I'm Lucy Greene," she introduces herself, then proceeds to give us all hugs and tell us how she missed us.

"Susan? What the hell is going on?" Adam asks, sounding more angry than confused now.

"She suffered an accident and... she lost her memory, Adam. She has amnesia."

"So?"

Susan shakes her head, her concerned gaze on her daughter the entire time. "She thinks you're still happily married."

The End

Cockamamie Unicorn Ramblings

Staring a new series is always scary for us. Especially after all the love The Baileys received, so we hope you enjoyed the start of The Greene Family series. We plotted this series out much like we did with The Baileys, trying to find tropes we haven't used yet, and later storylines we could weave into earlier books.

It's also exciting to start a new family! Especially when we only have to move over to the neighboring town.

As most of our readers know, we changed the name of this book from My Beautiful Nemesis to My Beautiful Neighbor. Cade just didn't come on the page like we expected him to. As Rayne wrote the rough draft she kept trying to get them to be enemies but she just wasn't feeling it. When Piper went through edits she called Rayne to say, "Um, they aren't enemies". She was right and so we changed the title to better reflect the story.

It goes to show even the best planning doesn't always work when you actually sit down to write the character. But if we would've reworked the story or changed Cade, it wouldn't have been authentic. We like our characters to talk to us as we explore them, almost like they're telling us who they are. So, although we LOVE the enemies-to-lovers trope, that wasn't Cade and Presley's story. Don't worry, it's someone else's. ;)

Once again, thank you to our tremendous team!

Danielle Sanchez and the entire Wildfire Marketing Solutions team.

Cassie from Joy Editing for line edits.

Ellie from My Brother's Editor for line edits.

Shawna from Behind the Writer for proofreading.

Hang Le for the cover and branding for the entire series.

Wander Aguiar for his awesome job of photographing our Cade and Presley.

Bloggers who consistently carve out time to read, review and/or promote us.

Piper Rayne Unicorns who made The Baileys so popular and love our characters like we do.

Readers who took the time to read our story when there's so many choices out there.

Adam's up next and yeah, we left you on a pretty heavy cliffy there for their story, leaving the question, "Why did Lucy walk out on Adam in the first place?" Good thing you don't have too long to wait! ;)

Lastly, we want to thank you for coming on this journey with us and being open to loving a new family. We know it takes trust in us to deliver a family you loved as much as the Baileys. So we hope this is a promising start! <3

We'd love for you to let us know who's story you're looking forward to in this family. Feel free to reach out to us on social media or via email. We love hearing from readers!

Xo,
    Piper & Rayne

ABOUT PIPER & RAYNE

Piper Rayne is a USA Today Bestselling Author duo who write "heartwarming humor with a side of sizzle" about families, whether that be blood or found. They both have e-readers full of one-clickable books, they're married to husbands who drive them to drink, and they're both chauffeurs to their kids. Most of all, they love hot heroes and quirky heroines who make them laugh, and they hope you do, too!

ALSO BY PIPER RAYNE

The Greenes

My Beautiful Neighbor

My Almost Ex

My Vegas Groom

The Baileys

Lessons from a One-Night Stand

Advice from a Jilted Bride

Birth of a Baby Daddy

Operation Bailey Wedding (Novella)

Falling for My Brother's Best Friend

Demise of a Self-Centered Playboy

Confessions of a Naughty Nanny

Operation Bailey Babies (Novella)

Secrets of the World's Worst Matchmaker

Winning My Best Friend's Girl

Rules for Dating your Ex

Operation Bailey Birthday (Novella)

The Modern Love World

Charmed by the Bartender

Hooked by the Boxer

Mad about the Banker

The Single Dad's Club

Real Deal

Dirty Talker

Sexy Beast

Hollywood Hearts

Mister Mom

Animal Attraction

Domestic Bliss

Bedroom Games

Cold as Ice

On Thin Ice

Break the Ice

Box Set

Charity Case

Manic Monday

Afternoon Delight

Happy Hour

Blue Collar Brothers

Flirting with Fire

Crushing on the Cop

Engaged to the EMT

White Collar Brothers

Sexy Filthy Boss

Dirty Flirty Enemy

Wild Steamy Hook-up

The Rooftop Crew

My Bestie's Ex

A Royal Mistake

The Rival Roomies

Our Star-Crossed Kiss

The Do-Over

A Co-Workers Crush

Hockey Hotties

My Lucky #13

The Trouble with #9

Faking it with #41

Made in the USA
Monee, IL
31 January 2022